OUR LADY CAME TO FATIMA

Our Lady Came to Fatima

Written by Ruth Fox Hume

ILLUSTRATED BY CHRISTOPHER J. PELICANO

IGNATIUS PRESS   SAN FRANCISCO

First edition published by Farrar, Straus & Cudahy, L.L.C., New York
Published with ecclesiastical approval

Cover art by Christopher J. Pelicano
Cover design by Riz Boncan Marsella

Published in 2005 by Ignatius Press, San Francisco
Published by arrangement with Farrar, Strauss and Giroux, L.L.C.
Library of Congress Control Number 2005927115
Manufactured by Thomson-Shore, Dexter, MI (USA); RMA155JM66, March, 2017 ∞

For
Paul, Michael, Ann, and Peter

CONTENTS

A Guide to Pronunciation

A "j" in Portuguese is pronounced like the "s" sound in *measure* or the "z" sound in *azure*. So the name Jacinta sounds like this: *Zhaceenta*; and the children's home village is Alzhus*trel*, with the emphasis on the italicized letters.

An "o" in the last syllable of a Portuguese word sounds like the "oo" in *boot*. Francisco's name is pronounced not *Franciscoh* but *Franciscoo*.

An "nh" is pronounced something like the "y" in *you*: Senhor—*Senyor*; Godinho—*Godeenyoo*; Valinhos—*Valeenyoos*.

Father Formigão's name is difficult to pronounce because there is no sound in English that is the exact equivalent. The curved line or tilda over the vowels shows that an *n* sound is there. It is like the French sound *on*. Say *Formignon*, but say it as though you were talking through your nose without quite finishing the *n* sound.

Prologue

The three children were playing in a flowering olive grove high on a hill overlooking the village. Suddenly a young man, brilliant as crystal in the rays of the sun, was standing before them. "Do not be afraid", he said. "I am the angel of peace. Pray with me!"

He knelt on the ground and said, "My God, I believe, I adore, I hope, and I love you. I ask forgiveness for those who do not believe, or adore, or hope, or love you!"

As he rose to his feet the angel said, "Pray in this way. The hearts of Jesus and Mary are ready to listen to you!"

Twice more the angel returned—in the summer and in the autumn. "You must pray," he said, "pray! The hearts of Jesus and Mary have merciful designs on you! Above all, bear and accept with patience the suffering God will send you."

What great plans were being made in heaven—plans so great that an angel had been sent to prepare the way for them?

And who were these three children on whom the eyes of God were already turned?

I

A LADY FROM HEAVEN

Lucia!" Maria called to her younger sister. "May I leave the baby here for an hour? I have to go get some needles."

"Oh, yes! Let me have her!" Lucia jumped off the well on which she had been standing, ran across the yard, and

held out her arms to her small niece. She planted a kiss
on the end of the baby's nose.

Maria looked into the yard and laughed. "I see you
have some company already! Sure the baby won't be too
much trouble?"

"Oh, no. We're playing May Procession. The baby
can march too—only I'll carry her. Everybody ready?"
she called to the dozen children in her care. "Let's start
marching! No—wait a minute! We have to make a
wreath for the baby, too!"

The older sister waved and went off on her errand.
There was never any reason to worry about the little
ones so long as Lucia was on the job!

Lucia was the most sought-after baby-sitter in the
whole village. The babies themselves loved her because
she made such a fuss over them. The toddlers flocked
around her like little sheep because she was so much
fun and could think up such lovely games to play. The
mothers of the village, on their way to the fields or the
grapevines, knew that they could just drop their children
off in the Santos' yard and the more the merrier as far
as Lucia was concerned.

"Now she's ready", Lucia exclaimed, clapping a
quickly made wreath on her niece's curly head. "Isabella,
you hold onto my skirt so you won't trip. Teresa, you be
the leader. Twice around the yard and then line up by
the tree."

Lucia could not honestly be described as a pretty girl.
Her nose was too flat and her mouth too large for that. If

she sometimes seemed more attractive than she really was, it was because her eyes were so bright and her face so full of fun. And she was so lively and happy. There was something about her that was as festive as the jingling earrings and jaunty velvet hat that she loved to wear to feast-day dances.

Lucia's family sometimes thought her a great nuisance because she was so affectionate. Families are like that in the Portuguese mountain country. They are loving, of course, but they are somehow unwilling to show it. The children grow up tough, independent, and ready for the life of hard work that lies ahead of them. There is a formality between them and their parents that is hard for us to understand. So when Lucia, as a little girl, would come dashing into the house and fling herself into her mother's arms, her older sisters always laughed at her, and her mother would mutter, half-pleased and half-annoyed, "Oh, here comes that little kissing-girl again!"

But the little ones of the village didn't find her affectionate ways a nuisance at all. Spending an afternoon with Lucia was almost as good as a holiday! When they grew tired of the imaginary holy-day processions she organized so well, Lucia could keep them happy for hours simply by talking. She knew more stories than any other girl in the village.

Lucia's fine collection of tales came to her in an unusual way. Her mother could read! This was a great accomplishment in the little village where entertainment certainly did not come ready-made.

Aljustrel was hardly a village at all. It was really a group of whitewashed houses clustered around the cobblestoned road that led south to Lisbon—and civilization. It was a kind of suburb of a not much larger village called Fatima. The only thing about Fatima that made it important was the fact that the church had been built there. This made it the parish center of the small farming villages that dot the slopes of the Serra da Aire, a rocky, windy mountain range in the exact center of Portugal.

Aljustrel is about a mile south of Fatima. There are hundreds of these little red-roofed communities sprinkled over the mountains, but it would be hard to find one less distinguished-looking than Aljustrel. In the 1910s it was a place of not the slightest interest to anyone in the world except the people who lived there. We can be reasonably certain that none of us would ever have heard its name if it had not been the birthplace of the girl named Lucia dos Santos and her two cousins, Francisco and Jacinta Marto.

Certainly the people of Aljustrel could see nothing unusual about Lucia and her cousins—up to the year 1917, that is. In that year the three children became quite a problem to the good citizens of Fatima and its suburbs.

Lucia had just turned ten. Francisco was within a month of being nine years old. His sister Jacinta was seven. Of all her friends and relatives in the village, Lucia loved these two little cousins best.

Their house was at the other end of the cobblestoned

street. It was a happy house. The family was prosperous, for Senhor Marto, whom everyone called "Ti", or "Uncle", was a hard-working, skillful farmer and the most respected man in the village. His wife, Olimpia, was a cheerful, easygoing, kindly woman. She was not very much like her stern, strong-minded sister-in-law, Lucia's mother.

Francisco and Jacinta were the youngest of the nine Marto children. What a handsome fellow Francisco was! He was tall, straight, and surefooted. Day or night he loved to roam the rocky mountaintops, on the lookout for strange animals. These, to the distress of his mother, he frequently brought home in his pockets and kept as pets. Lizards, snakes, rabbits, moles, newts—you never could tell what Francisco would turn up with next.

There was one thing about Francisco that Lucia could not understand. He was a brave fox hunter and snake tamer, but he hated fighting. He was not a coward; it was just that the ordinary arguing and scuffling of the children of the village seemed silly to him.

Unlike most boys of his age, Francisco could never work up a strong, fighting sense of ownership. One day his faithful godmother brought him a present as a souvenir of her yearly trip to the beach. It was only a cheap little handkerchief, stamped with a picture of Our Lady of Nazaré, but Francisco loved it dearly. A few days later the handkerchief mysteriously disappeared. Francisco's friends put their heads together and tried to figure out the facts of the case. The handkerchief must have been stolen—and they had a pretty good idea who might have stolen it. They investigated by rather stern police methods. Sure enough, when the suspect had been pinned to the ground and searched, the evidence was found in his pocket.

"It's mine", the culprit whined, kicking and struggling to get up. "It's mine! I didn't take his. I had one, too!" This was sheer nonsense. Francisco's unique souvenir of the boardwalk at Nazaré had been the wonder of the village children. But to the utter amazement of his friends, Francisco turned away, saying, "Let him keep it if he wants it so badly. I don't mind."

Sometimes, the boys in the village thought, it was hard to figure out Francisco! They would find it harder still before the year was over.

Francisco's little sister, Jacinta, was the pet of the family, and not only because she was the youngest. She was a lovely little thing with large eyes and beautiful features. She was as graceful as a hummingbird and almost as active, for she much preferred running to walking, and dancing to running. She was so gentle and affectionate that everyone in the village loved her. But Jacinta was no picture-book saint, waiting to have her halo colored in yellow crayon. She had a sweet disposition, but she also had a strong will that went into instant action whenever a game was not played strictly according to her rules.

Unlike her brother, Jacinta had a strong sense of possession—too strong. It always showed up during a round of "buttons", the game the children liked best. Like marbles, "buttons" was a game of skill, but the forfeit was more serious. If the loser ran out of spares, he simply ripped the buttons off his clothes and threw them into the pot. "Buttons" was a dangerous game to play for keeps, but this, unfortunately, was the only way Jacinta liked to play it. Since Jacinta was an expert, Lucia often had to go home to supper with her buttonless dress flapping open down her back. Lucia's mother saw nothing the least bit funny about this. She had enough to do around the house without searching for replacements to sew on her daughter's dress! Lucia was torn between her sporting instinct and her fear of being spanked for lack of buttons. Only when she threatened to give up the game forever did Jacinta agree to a change in the rules.

Lucia may have been spirited and fun-loving, but she was really much more grown-up than most American girls her age. When she was nine years old, one of the most important jobs of the family was handed over to her. She became the shepherdess of the flock. It was a big job for a nine-year-old, but Lucia was up to it. Besides, she knew that her parents needed all the help she could give them. Trying to make a living out of that rocky land was heartbreaking work. It took all the muscle that Lucia's father and brothers could put into it. Besides struggling with his own land, Lucia's father was overseer for a wealthy landowner of the region. And to add a little more to the family income, the older girls took in sewing, at which they were expert. This left the care of the sheep entirely in the capable hands of young Lucia.

There was, of course, no interruption by school. No one had ever thought of sending Lucia to school. What *for*? Boys were the only ones who needed any schooling, her family thought.

Although Lucia herself was proud of her new chores, her young cousins objected strenuously, particularly Jacinta. "What will *I* do all day while Lucia is off tending a bunch of silly sheep?" wailed the little girl.

She raised such a fuss that her mother finally thought of a solution. "If Jacinta wants to play shepherdess, too," Tia Olimpia said one day to her husband, "let her. She can take a few of our sheep and go along with Lucia."

"Me, too?" Francisco asked hopefully.

"All right—if you promise to get to school on time!"

The young Martos were delighted with the idea. This was even better than playing with Lucia at home and having to share her with a yardful of visiting babies.

In the much-too-short spring that separated the freezing winters of the Serra from its broiling summers, the sheep were kept out to pasture all day long. Jacinta loved to be outdoors in the wild hills while the sheep grazed so safely in the care of three shepherds. She loved to climb to the highest peak of the Serra and make the echo answer her from across the valley. Of all the words that made good echoes, the one Jacinta liked best was "Maria".

The other shepherds on the lower slopes could hear her clear voice chasing itself across the lonely mountaintops. "Ma–*ri*–a! Ma–*riiii*–a!"

Most of all Jacinta loved her sheep. She always gave names to the new lambs—"Dove", "Star", "Beauty", "Snow"—and, regardless of how her own little legs felt by the end of the day, she would gladly carry the smallest lamb home in the evening if she thought its legs were tired.

The long hours in the hills passed quickly. Sometimes Lucia told stories from her mother's wonderful, mysterious books. The two little ones loved the stories of the saints, and especially stories from the life of our Lord. Jacinta could never hear Lucia tell about the Passion without bursting into tears. "Poor Jesus," she would say from the depths of her tender heart, "I will never sin and make you sad again!"

Sometimes Francisco would play his reed pipe, while the girls danced. Sometimes they searched for honey in likely looking tree stumps, or built playhouses out of stone. And thus they lived the peaceful, uneventful life that was changed in the summer of 1916 by three visits from an angel.

Not that the angel in any way changed the outer appearance of their lives. No one in the village knew anything about it at all. The children had been so overwhelmed by the angel's presence that, even if they had wanted to, they could not have talked about it to anyone else. They did not understand exactly what the angel's visits meant, but they felt, without knowing why, that he had come in preparation for something else.

For what?

They did not know. They kept the angel's words in their hearts and waited.

On the Sunday before Ascension, slightly more than a year after the first visit of the angel, the three friends went to early Mass in the parish church at Fatima. Then they hurried home to get the sheep out to pasture. It had been a dry week. Lucia looked for grazing land with moist grass.

About two miles west of Fatima, on one of the highest slopes of the Serra, there was a flat field called the Cova da Iria, where Lucia's father owned a plot of farmland. When rainwater ran off the mountains, it always collected in the Cova.

Here the shepherds brought their flocks shortly before noon on the morning of May 13, 1917. When the sheep were happily pastured in the dewy grass, the three friends sat down near a small azinheira tree about five feet tall—one of the sturdy little holm oaks that provide the people of the mountains with their finest building wood. They ate their lunch of bread, cheese, and Sunday fruits, and then, as was their custom after lunch, they said the Rosary.

Their version of the Rosary was, to say the least, condensed. At times it had seemed a little long to them. They had fallen into the habit of shortening it, bit by bit, until nothing was left but the first words of each prayer, followed by a short pause: "Our Father . . . Hail Mary . . . Hail Mary . . . Hail Mary . . . Hail Mary

... Hail Mary... Hail Mary... Hail Mary... Hail Mary... Hail Mary... Hail Mary... Glory be to the Father..." And the decade was over.

When they had finished their streamlined prayers, Jacinta said, "What shall we play first?"

"Let's build a stone house!" Francisco suggested.

"That's a good idea. Let's make a big one!" Jacinta jumped up and ran down the slope to a little heap of the oddly shaped rocks that were scattered all over the field.

"You girls collect the stones. *I*'ll do the building", Francisco said briskly.

"Here's a flat one for the floor", Lucia began, then she stopped talking and blinked after the flash of light that had darted across the blue sky. "Was that lightning?" she asked.

"Yes—but why? It's such a nice day", Francisco said.

"I guess a storm's coming up! We'd better start home."

Reluctantly, the boy let the stone roll out of his hand. "I don't see how it can storm when the sun is shining", he muttered, as he followed the girls down the slope toward the flock.

Another flash of lightning streaked across the sky. This time the three shepherds began to run in earnest to get the sheep. As they passed the glossy-leaved azinheira, they stopped short and stared as if they could not possibly believe what they were seeing, even though what they were seeing was perfectly clear.

They were no longer alone in the field. A young lady—she looked no more than sixteen or seventeen—was standing on the branches of the tree, looking down at them thoughtfully. The children stared at her, absolutely dumbfounded.

The girl on the oak tree was radiantly, luminously beautiful. She seemed to be made entirely of light, so brilliant that it almost hurt to look at her. She wore a long white veil and a simple white gown. Around her neck she wore a slender cord that ended in a small pendant of golden light. There was a rosary in her hands, and it glowed like the stars of the summer sky.

"Please don't be afraid of me", she said in a melodious voice. "I won't hurt you."

Lucia realized that she was, in fact, not the least bit afraid any more. "Where do you come from?" she asked the Lady.

"I come from heaven."

This did not surprise Lucia, as it seemed unlikely that so radiant a creature could have come from any place else. "And what do you want of me?" Her heart was pounding with excitement.

"I want you to return here at the very same hour on the thirteenth of each month for the next six months", the Lady said. "Later I shall tell you who I am and what it is I most desire."

"And shall I go to heaven?" Lucia asked impulsively.

"Yes, you will."

"And Jacinta?"

"Jacinta, too."

"And Francisco?"

The Lady looked thoughtfully at the little boy, her face a shade more serious than it had been. "Francisco, too. But first he will have to say many Rosaries."

Francisco looked back at the Lady in rapt admiration, but for the moment her advice was lost on him. Although he knew that she was talking with Lucia, he himself could not hear a word she said. He heard Lucia ask about some friends of hers who had died that year, and then he saw the Lady bend forward a little farther and say something very earnestly.

What she said was this: "Will you offer yourselves to God and bear all the sufferings he sends you, in atonement for all the sins that offend him, and for the conversion of sinners?"

"Oh, we will! We will!" Lucia replied eagerly.

"Then," said the Lady, "you will have a great deal to suffer!" How many times during the coming year Lucia would remember those words! "But the grace of God will be with you and will strengthen you!"

As she said this, the Lady opened her hands and floods of light streamed out of them. The children were surrounded by an indescribable radiance that made them understand exactly what she meant when she spoke of the grace of God. They fell to their knees.

"Say the Rosary every day," the Lady said, "to bring peace to the world and an end to the war." Then she began to rise slowly from the tree and disappear into the eastern sky, leaving a slow-fading trail of light behind her.

For a long moment the three children simply stared after her, unable to speak or to move. "Oh," Jacinta whispered at last, "what a beautiful Lady!"

Then they began to talk, everyone at once. They felt almost dizzy with happiness. The angel had left them exhausted and overpowered, unable to say very much about their experience—even to each other. The Lady left them so full of lightness and joy that they felt as though they could not talk fast enough about her.

First Lucia and Jacinta had to tell Francisco about the whole conversation, for he had not heard the Lady speak. Then they had to go over every detail of the Lady's dress and appearance. But suddenly Lucia interrupted the raptures of Jacinta to say sharply, "You mustn't say a word about this to anyone else, do you understand?"

"Oh, no! I won't!" the little girl promised, still bubbling. "I won't tell a soul! Not even Mother!"

"Let's go home now." Lucia stood up. "And don't forget," she repeatedly firmly, "we're not going to tell anyone!"

"No one! I promise!"

"Well—then try to *look* as though nothing had happened, too!" Lucia said, almost crossly, for Jacinta's face alone would have given away the secret.

The shepherds drove the flock down the rocky slopes of the mountain and out onto the narrow path to Aljustrel. Lucia did not even hear the happy chatter of

Jacinta as they walked home. She was thinking. She could hear the Lady's voice as clearly as she had heard it an hour before.

"Will you offer yourselves to God and bear all the sufferings he sends you?"

She did not know exactly how the Lady's words would be realized. But one thing she knew beyond a shadow of a doubt—that life as she had known it was over now. It had ended as suddenly as the flash of lightning that had announced the visitor from heaven.

2

A CRISIS IN THE FAMILY

WHEN THEY REACHED the village, the children
separated. Lucia drove her sheep into their corral. Francisco disappeared around a corner. He was eager
for a moment of quiet in which to be with his own
thoughts. Left alone, Jacinta ran into her house and
called her mother.

Her Uncle Antonio Silva was having a quiet nap in the kitchen. "Your mother and father went to the fair at Batalha to buy a pig", he said, half awake, and closed his eyes again.

Jacinta went outside and moped around the front door, waiting. The longer she waited, the more certain she felt that unless she could talk to someone soon, she would burst with bottled-up excitement. By the time she finally caught sight of her mother and father, she had forgotten all about her promise to Lucia. She ran down the street to meet them and flung her arms around her mother's skirts.

"Oh, Mother", she said, looking up into the smiling face. "I saw our Lady today in the Cova da Iria!"

Tia Olimpia had spent a long, hot afternoon herding a squealing baby pig down the dusty road from Batalha. The smile faded. "That's likely!" she said sourly, as she trudged wearily up the front steps. "You're such a good little saint that you can see our Lady now!"

"But I *did* see her!" Jacinta followed her mother into the kitchen. "So did Lucia and Francisco. And Lucia even *talked* to her! Oh, Mother, she was so beautiful! She was all made of light, and she said we should say the Rosary every day, and she said we would all go to heaven, and she said . . ."

"John! Help your father get the pig into the pen! Antonio, take these husks out back. That animal must be starving by now. Jacinta, stop chattering and start stirring up the soup, child! Don't just stand there!" And Tia

Olimpia flounced out of the kitchen into the yard to check on the important new addition to the household.

But when the baby pig had been settled for the night and the family had finally gathered around its cabbage soup and potatoes, Tia Olimpia's usual jolly spirits returned. "*Now*, Jacinta," she said, "tell Father that pretty story you told me about the Lady in the Cova da Iria."

The little girl's face brightened at once.

"What story did she tell you?" Francisco began.

But Jacinta paid no attention at all to her scowling brother. Talking as fast as she could talk, she began at the beginning and told it all to the very end . . . "And when she went back to heaven, the doors seemed to shut so quickly that I thought her feet would get caught!"

The Martos were a jolly, affectionate family, so the laughter and joking that greeted this tale were good-natured. Even the hoots of her big brothers were touched with admiration. Jacinta could certainly make up a good yarn when she put her mind to it! Her sisters were full of questions about the mysterious lady's dress and veil and jewelry. In the hubbub of excited questions and comments only one person was silent. Ti Marto was a rare man. He thought before he spoke. At last he interrupted the noise to say, "Francisco, is this true?"

The boy nodded. "It's all true", he said, glowering at his talkative sister. "But she wasn't supposed to tell! She promised! Girls just can't keep *anything* to themselves!"

The chattering began again, but Ti Marto did not hear it. He was thinking: "Our Lady has appeared on earth before—and often to children. My children are not unusual children, but they are good children. Besides, they have never told lies before, so why should they tell such a big one now? If they say it is all the truth, then it *must* be the truth."

". . . It is a lie! I say it is a lie! *Ai!* All my life I have made my children tell the truth! Now in my old age my daughter tells me not only lies, but sacrilegious lies as well!"

Maria Rosa Santos' fierce eyes peered into her daughter's sad ones. "It is a lie!" she repeated.

"It's the truth, Mother, but I didn't want you to know about it. . . ."

It was Monday morning. Word had traveled by a direct route—from Senhora Marto, to the Martos' nearest neighbor, to Lucia's sister, to Lucia's mother. And Lucia's mother was outraged.

Now Maria Rosa, stern as she often seemed to her children, was really a very good, pious woman. She had many virtues, but she was a little short on simple human kindness. And she had no imagination whatsoever. Her mind was already made up. Lucia had invented a fantastic story—one that would make her family's name a joke from one end of the village to the other. Maria Rosa regarded lying as a sin second only to murder. She set her square jaw and said, "You'll take it back yet, my girl! I promise you that!"

In a place the size of Aljustrel a story so fantastic did not take long to spread. By the time the children were

ready to take the sheep to pasture that morning, almost
everyone they met had heard it. A stream of rude comments followed them out of the village.

"Hey, Lucia! Remember me to our Lady when you
see her again!"

"Ask her to come over and fix my roof instead of
walking around on trees!"

"Come and see us before you leave for heaven!"

Most of these remarks were directed at Lucia. Everyone assumed that she was the ringleader and that the
featherheaded little Martos were simply saying what she
told them to say. At each new gibe, a large tear of
remorse trickled off the end of Jacinta's nose. It was all
her fault! By the time they reached the Cova, the little
girl was so gloomy that even Lucia began to feel sorry for
her. "Don't fret, Jacinta", she said. "I'm not angry with
you."

"But you're in so much trouble, Lucia!"

"And all because you couldn't keep quiet!" Francisco
muttered, in the critical tone of big brothers the world
over.

"But it's done now. You can't make it better by crying.
Come on, we'll play. Do you want to finish the stone
house?"

Jacinta wiped the last tear from her eyes joyfully. But
she made no move to get up and play. "I don't feel like
playing, Lucia. I'm thinking about the Lady. I was
wondering about something she said."

"What, Jacinta?"

"She told us to say the Rosary every day. Well—I'm sure she meant the *whole* Rosary, not just the first few words of every prayer. Just saying 'Our Father, Hail Mary, Hail Mary, Hail Mary, Hail Mary' is cheating, you know!"

They nodded solemnly, suddenly ashamed. It seemed a very low kind of cheating to them now, in view of the fact that our Lady herself had come all the way from heaven to tell them to say the Rosary.

"And she said we should make sacrifices for sinners. Think of some sacrifice we could make, Lucia."

Lucia thought. Before she could come up with an answer, Francisco said, "We could give our lunches to the sheep!"

The girls looked at him, amazed by so direct an approach to this strange, new problem.

"Well, we're hungry, aren't we?" he said. "So it would be a sacrifice, wouldn't it? Come on!" And he marched manfully toward the lucky flock, opening his lunch bag as he went.

They ate green acorns for lunch that day and every day after that. Unfortunately for the sheep, they soon decided that it would be better to give the lunches their mothers packed to the poor children who lived on the outskirts of the village.

But eating acorns and roots for lunch soon proved to be by far the least painful of the sacrifices they were able to offer for sinners. Within a few days word had spread from Aljustrel to Fatima, the parish center. In due course it reached the eager ears of Francisco's teacher and schoolmates. They promptly proceeded to make Francisco's school life miserable. But the boy could look forward to holidays, at least, or to the coming summer vacation, or to the days when he played hooky and spent the school hours happily kneeling before the Blessed Sacrament.

For Lucia there was no escape. It was in her own home that she found her greatest sorrows. All day and all night too, it seemed to her, Maria Rosa brooded over the situation. One morning, after an hour of threats, bribes, and tears, she finally seized the broom and beat the unhappy girl with it as hard as she could. During all this Lucia did not say a word. Her silence simply enraged her mother more.

"Get off with the sheep now", Maria Rosa said. "But if you don't confess by tonight, you will be even sorrier than you are now!"

When she met her cousins that day, Lucia was weeping bitterly. "What am I going to do?" she asked them. "Mother says I have to say I lied! But how can I?"

Francisco's eyes filled with tears at the sight of Lucia's. He turned to Jacinta and said, "It's all because you couldn't keep quiet!"

"Oh, Lucia!" The little girl was again filled with remorse. "Please forgive me! I'll never tell anything to anybody again, so long as I live!"

But Maria Rosa was as unhappy as her daughter that morning. When the girl left with the sheep, the mother seized her shawl and rushed out of the house in the direction of Fatima. She had carried the burden by herself long enough. Now she needed the advice of an expert.

The pastor of Fatima was a big, bluff, outspoken man. Like most people in the parish, Maria Rosa was a little afraid of him. Although she dreaded the thought of having to tell him the disgraceful tale, she was sure that he would think of some practical answer to it. He was a man who had no use at all for nonsense!

Father Ferreira had already heard the story. To Maria Rosa's surprise, he took it much less seriously than she. When she told him, with some pride, about the events of the morning, he frowned and shook his bushy head. "Listen, my dear lady," he said, "you have eight children, and you know so little about them. Don't you realize that girls of Lucia's age do things like this for attention? Stop fussing at her so much. Ignore her. And, for heaven's sakes, don't beat the poor girl again."

He thought for a moment. "When did you say she's supposed to meet this vision again?"

"On the thirteenth of June, Reverend Father."

The priest laughed. "Those children won't be skulking around the Cova da Iria at noon on the thirteenth of June, woman! Think what day it is!"

For the first time in two weeks Maria Rosa's broad face softened into a wide grin. "Of course! I forgot. Saint Anthony!"

June 13! The *festa* of Saint Anthony! The mere

thought of it was enough to send happy chills up the spines of the parish children! There is nothing in this country comparable to the celebration of a favorite saint's day in a small European village. And Saint Anthony was the undisputed favorite in Fatima. The Italians might call him "Saint Anthony of Padua" all they liked, but the fact remained that he had been born in Lisbon, Portugal!

The thirteenth of June produced a feeling like a combination Christmas and the Fourth of July. Maria Rosa knew that few children in the village looked forward to the *festa* more eagerly than her youngest daughter. Everything about it delighted Lucia, from the High Mass to the brass band that played for the annual Saint Anthony's day parade. A girl who loved to get dressed up and have fun and dance as much as Lucia did would not miss the greatest day in the year just for the sake of keeping up a rather poor joke about seeing a Lady on top of a tree! The mother felt better than she had felt since the fourteenth of May. Father Ferreira had been right. She *was* taking this business too seriously. Saint Anthony would put an end to it on the thirteenth of June!

3

A MESSAGE FOR MARIA ROSA

MARIA ROSA went to work on her plan with gusto. First she gathered her older children into the kitchen for a council of war. "From now on," she said briskly, "we won't even mention this business in the Cova. We'll just keep talking and talking about the *festa*!"

And talk she did. "I hear they're having three extra pieces in the band this year!" Maria Rosa would say cheerfully. Or, "I've pressed your good white kerchief, Lucia, so it will be all ready for the *festa!*"

Lucia's brothers and sisters got into the spirit of the game, too, for they were tired of their mother's wailing over the evil ways of their pesky little sister. "The fireworks got here from Lisbon today!" Lucia's brother told her gleefully. "They say there are twice as many as last year!"

"Only a week. . . . Only three days. . . . Only a day to the thirteenth!" her sister Gloria said each evening at dinner. "I can hardly wait!"

Lucia, too, could hardly wait for the great day, but there was scarcely a thought in her mind for her old friend, Saint Anthony. To the three children the thirteenth of June meant only one thing—the Lady would be back!

The day arrived at last—beautiful, bright, and cloudless. The shepherds took their flocks out for feeding just after sunrise so that they would be finished working in time to get to eight o'clock Mass. When the sheep were back in the corral, Lucia ran into the house and began to get dressed in her Sunday clothes. Her *festa* clothes, Maria Rosa noted with secret rejoicing, as she watched her daughter leave for Fatima. She was going early, Lucia told her, to meet some of the girls with whom she had made her First Communion.

That settled it, Maria Rosa thought. Once Lucia got

to Fatima and saw the flags and the bunting, and the brightly decorated carts, and the bandstand, and the fireworks piled high in the square—well, she would simply stay there all day. Her friends would persuade her to stay, even if her mother could not, Maria Rosa mused sourly. These girls were all older than Lucia and should be able to talk some sense into her. Maria Rosa thought back to the day of Lucia's First Communion. She sighed briefly, allowing herself a moment of self-pity. She had been so proud of Lucia that day.

Since the thirteenth of May, Lucia, too, had thought back on that wonderful day four years ago. She had been six at the time, but for some reason she had taken it into her head that she wanted to make her First Communion that year and no other! Her mother saw nothing wrong with the idea. It was true that the age of the regular First Communion class was nine or ten, but had not the Pope, the saintly Pius X, decreed that children could receive the sacraments when they reached "the age of reason" ? Lucia had plenty of sense, Maria Rosa thought, and she knew her catechism forward and backward. The day before the ceremony, she had presented her daughter to the pastor with the request that the child be put through the same test as the First Communion class.

The surprised priest agreed and proceeded with the standard questions: "Who made the world? Why did God make you? Did God have any beginning?" Lucia was nervous, but she kept her wits about her and answered perfectly. The good priest was undecided about what to do. He thought a minute and said, "She answers very well, but she is a little young. Even according to the new regulations, seven is about the youngest . . ." He was stopped by the look of tragic disappointment on the little girl's face. "Next year", he finished lamely. "Let's just wait until next year."

Lucia went out of the sacristy into the church, put her head on her arm, and burst into tears. Her mother sat beside her, helpless. She could think of nothing to do or say.

Suddenly Lucia felt a hand on her shoulder. She looked up and saw a strange priest looking down at her. It was a famous Jesuit preacher named Father Cruz, a great man in the battle between the Church and the hostile government. He was risking prison by staying in the country. Chance had brought him to Fatima to preach a three-day mission. He asked Lucia what was bothering her. Between sobs, she told him. The priest clucked sympathetically and said, "Well, don't cry any more. Let's talk about it." He sat down next to her and began to ask questions. After several minutes of this, he excused himself, marched into the sacristy, and said to the astonished pastor, "That child out there is perfectly ready for the sacraments. Why not let her go to Communion tomorrow?"

The pastor shrugged his agreement. What could he do if his distinguished visitor wanted it that way? Thus it happened that the saintly Jesuit was the first confessor Lucia ever had.

Next day she was so excited that she could hardly stand still long enough to let her sisters dress her. Before Mass began, she knelt in front of the statue of our Lady and looked up into the serene face. "Please keep my poor heart for God", she said. "Make me a saint." It seemed to the charmed eye of the little girl that the statue smiled and nodded at her gently. She had wondered about it often since then.

Poor Maria Rosa! Her optimistic mood lasted only a few hours. She had overlooked the important fact that Lucia was the one who usually did the persuading in her crowd, even though she was the youngest. By the time the girls came out of church, the matter was settled. Lucia was not going to the *festa* with them. They were going to the Cova with her!

To the children's surprise, a small crowd of people— perhaps fifty—had gathered there to meet them. Most of them were from neighboring villages. Among them was a woman from Moita named Maria Carreira, who had come with her crippled son, John. Lucia looked over the little group, half suspiciously. Had they come to see how big a laugh they could get? No, surely they would not miss all the fun now going on at the parade just for that. Did they really believe that something was going to happen, then? Lucia felt a great stab of bitterness. These strangers were looking at her with a great deal of interest and respect. Most of them were already kneeling down and getting out their rosary beads. Yet her own family had not once so much as whispered the thought that perhaps she was telling the truth after all!

The children sat down to wait. One of Lucia's friends began to say the Rosary. Everyone joined in. When it was over, Lucia anxiously peered into the sky. As the eager friend launched into the litany of our Lady, Lucia said, "Wait—there won't be time! Jacinta! Do you see it?"

There was a flash of lightning. The three children ran toward the oak tree and fell to their knees.

The Lady had come back, as she had promised. There she stood, bending down a little from the top of the tree, looking down at them with love, and with sadness, too. All the bitterness of the past weeks melted from Lucia's soul like ice in the sun.

The Lady waited for Lucia to speak. "Please tell me what you want of me", the girl asked, when she had found her voice.

"I want you to come here on the thirteenth of next month", the Lady said. "I want you to continue saying the Rosary every day. And after each one of the mysteries, I want you to pray in this way: *O my Jesus, forgive us our sins and save us from the fires of hell! Take all souls to heaven, especially those who are most in need of your mercy!* I want you to learn how to read and write. Later I will tell you what else I want of you."

Even in the dazzling joy of the moment Lucia did not forget to tell the Lady about a sick woman for whom she had been asked to pray. Then she said hopefully, "Will you *please* take us to heaven with you?" How simple it would make everything!

The Lady looked lovingly at the two little ones. "I shall take Jacinta and Francisco—soon. But you," she said, turning back to Lucia, "must remain a little longer because Jesus wishes you to make me known and loved on earth. He wishes you to establish devotion in the world to my Immaculate Heart."

"Must I remain in the world alone?" Lucia asked, half reproachfully.

"Not alone, my child. And you must not be sad. I will be with you always, and my Immaculate Heart will be your comfort and the way that will lead you to God."

Again the Lady opened her hands, and again the light of heaven streamed around the children. Close to her right hand they saw a heart, surrounded by thorns. The Immaculate Heart of Mary! As they gazed at the radiant image, the Lady rose from the tree and glided quickly to the east. "There," Lucia said, looking after her until the last glimmer of her sun-woven dress had disappeared, "now we can't see her any more. She's gone back to heaven!"

Maria Carreira and the others hurried into Fatima, where they found all their friends and relatives conveniently gathered in one place. Within ten minutes everyone in the parish knew what had happened in the Cova da Iria that afternoon. Maria Carreira and a few others told the story with a burning faith that it really had happened. The story spread like a brush fire. The faith did not.

Maria Rosa was kneading dough and was, for the moment, silent. She had not been silent for very long during the past week, so Lucia had not had the smallest chance to deliver that part of the Lady's message which required the help of her parents.

There was no point in waiting for the right moment, Lucia decided. No moment would be right for this message. She slipped into the kitchen and sat down behind her mother. "Mother, could I please go to school and learn to read and write?" she blurted in the direction of the unfriendly back.

Maria Rosa dropped the lump of dough and turned around slowly. "You want to go to school and learn to read and write?" she repeated in a tight, small voice.

Lucia's face grew hot. "The—the Lady told me to", she said weakly.

Maria Rosa sat down beside the hearth and stared at the girl. This was more than she had expected. That her daughter should make up stories about seeing a Lady from heaven was bad enough. That this mythical Lady from heaven was now giving orders to the family was simply too much. Why, the girl must be out of her mind to think that she could get away with this! The idea frightened Maria Rosa. Maybe her daughter really *was* going crazy. "Now!" she said, her voice rising sharply. "Now we're going to see the end of this! To-morrow we go to see the pastor. You'll tell *him* the truth or you'll be sorrier than you've ever been in your whole life!"

4

A CASE OF MISTAKEN IDENTITY

BUT MY DEAR CHILD, can you give me one good reason why this Lady of yours should have come down all the way from heaven to tell the people of the parish to say the Rosary every day? Practically everybody in Fatima says the Rosary every day already!"

Father Ferreira was a huge man with a deep, booming voice. As she looked up at him, Lucia thought that he must be at least twelve feet tall. Her knees quaked. But the pastor was a good man, too, whose duty it was to keep the souls in his care out of as much trouble as he could. And this little girl seemed to be looking for a great deal of trouble.

Lucia lowered her eyes. "I don't know, Reverend Father. But that's what she said."

Father Ferreira sighed. He had sworn to himself that he would keep his temper, no matter what happened. "Well, did this Lady give any other reason for making the trip?"

Lucia bit her lip. What could she say to him? *Yes, Father, she has chosen me, Lucia dos Santos, to establish in the world a devotion to the Immaculate Heart of Mary!* Her face grew hot at the very thought of it. No wonder the Lady had made them all realize, even without words, that this part of her message should remain a secret for the time being.

Lucia did not know how to turn aside a direct question. She said, "Yes, Father, she did. But I can't tell you."

"What do you mean? That this thing—this Lady—told you a secret?" Lucia nodded.

"But certainly you can tell the secret to your own pastor!"

Lucia only shook her head. The priest began to worry. There was perhaps more here than a girl trying to attract attention. He felt sure that he could have spotted a lie within five minutes of conversation. He realized with a sinking feeling in his heart that the girl was probably telling what she thought was the truth.

"My dear child . . ." He stood up and walked around the desk. "My dear child, God *has* been known to send messages to earth by means of some chosen soul. That is perfectly true. But the person chosen has always been told to confide the message to someone else—someone in authority who can do something about it. Now you claim to have a secret from our Lady that you won't even tell your own pastor!" He bent over so that his face was directly opposite hers. "If you are not lying—and I do not believe that you are—if you really did see some Lady in white there at the Cova, then I have to warn you that she might very well be sent there by the devil!"

There was a gasp of horror from the other side of the room where Maria Rosa stood like doom in the doorway. The devil! It was the one thought that had not yet crossed her mind.

Until that day it had not crossed Lucia's mind, either. But now she could not get free of it. Of course it was possible! It was, in fact, very likely. The devil was an expert at making just the kind of trouble that had been brewing in Aljustrel ever since the thirteenth of May—discord, quarreling, doubts, scandal.

Lucia suffered this misery as long as she could before she finally broke down and told Jacinta and Francisco what was on her mind. Jacinta's beautiful big eyes widened. "Oh, Lucia! Don't say that! Why, the devil is ugly and lives in hell! But the Lady is beautiful, and you know we saw her go up into heaven!"

Francisco found this simple argument perfectly convincing. "Now look, Lucia", he said firmly to the older girl. "Why should we be afraid of anything? The Lady is our friend, and she said she would help us!"

But Lucia walked in vague fear by day and slept in actual terror by night, when vivid dreams of the laughing devil terrified her. While she had been happy and secure in her knowledge of the Lady's love, she had willingly accepted the abuse of her family and neighbors. But now, "What for?" she asked herself. "Why should I go on like this? One little lie and it's all over."

"I'm going to tell them I made it all up", she said to her cousins one day.

"Lucia! Lucia! You can't do that!" Jacinta cried. "How can you say we didn't see her when you know perfectly well we did? It would be a terrible lie!"

"What's the difference? They all say I'm a liar anyway!"

But as many times as she tried, she could never actually bring herself to deny the Lady.

Life went on in this unhappy way until the twelfth of July, the eve of the next visit. The three friends were sitting by the well where the angel had once stood. Jacinta and Francisco were chattering happily about the next day. "Lucia," asked the little girl, "tomorrow will you please tell our Lady that we . . ."

"I can't tell her anything", Lucia interrupted. "I'm not going to the Cova tomorrow!"

There was a moment of stunned silence. Then Francisco said, "But—but you *have* to go, Lucia!"

"Well, I'm *not!*"

Jacinta clenched her small fists in honest indignation. "Well, if you won't go, I'll—I'll just talk to the Lady myself! But Lucia . . ." She suddenly burst into tears. "What shall I tell her when she asks me where you are?"

"Tell her I'm afraid she comes from the devil!" Lucia answered and ran home as fast as she could.

She went about her chores the next morning as though she were made of lead. Her eyes were heavy after a troubled night. She did not even see the look of smug delight on her mother's face as Maria Rosa began to realize that her daughter was not planning to go to the Cova today.

But a little after eleven o'clock—as quickly as one second becomes the next—it was all over. Lucia looked around for her fear and found that it was gone. She did not know why her doubts had left her so suddenly. She only knew that she felt as though every mountain in Portugal had been lifted off her shoulders.

"You will have much to suffer, but the grace of God will be with you and strengthen you!" The grace of God had indeed been with her. Lucia, who had been too honest to tell the one lie that would have made people stop calling her a liar, had driven the devils out of her head

forever. She would never again suffer from doubts of any kind.

Lucia rushed out of the house and ran over to the Martos' home. "I'm coming with you", she called as she burst into her cousins' room. "Wait for me!"

"Oh, Lucia!" Jacinta and Francisco were kneeling by the bed. The little girl's eyes were red. "We *are* waiting for you. We've been praying all night that you would come. We didn't have the nerve to go without you!"

"Well, let's go, then!" Lucia said, laughing for the first time in weeks. "What are you waiting for? Come on!" And she flew over the one and a half miles that separated her from the Lady as though she were made of air.

Tia Olimpia had been secretly relieved when Jacinta and Francisco told her that they would not go to meet the Lady that day because Lucia would not go with them. The whole thing was beyond her. She was glad to see the end of it.

So when she heard the children run out of the house, a sudden, unreasoning fear seized her. She rushed to her sister-in-law's house in a panic. "Maria Rosa! They've gone to the Cova after all! Lucia came and got them!"

Lucia's mother put down her mop and wiped her forehead. "She went? Lucia? But I thought she was out in the yard. *Ai*, that wretched girl! She was just trying to fool me all along!"

"Let's go after them! Something dreadful might happen!"

"Calm down, Olimpia." Maria Rosa took off her

apron. "If you want me to go with you, I'll go. But try to keep your face covered. I don't want anyone to know we're there." She flung a shawl around her head and followed Tia Olimpia out of the house.

The two women traveled by a back path unknown to the out-of-town people. When they reached the Cova, they ducked behind a rock and peeped out over the crowd. *"Ai!"* Maria muttered, "Look at them all! The fools! What do they expect to see?"

Nearly three thousand pilgrims were gathered. Olimpia made a quick sign of the cross. She had never seen so many people together in one place. "Where are the children?" she whispered fearfully.

Maria Rosa scanned the crowd. "Down there—by the tree where they say she stands." Her voice was scornful. "And—Ai!—look who is standing right next to them in plain sight!"

Olimpia popped up from behind the rock, pulling her shawl more closely about her head, and looked. Ti Marto was standing by the azinheira, in the very center of the crowd, keeping a watchful eye on his children. His rosary was in his hand, and he was saying it along with the others.

"Why does he appear openly?" Maria Rosa muttered angrily. "Now people will say that the parents are encouraging them. . ."

"But, but, he *believes* them", Olimpia moaned. It was all too much for her.

When the Rosary was finished, Ti Marto put his

beads into his pocket and looked around. The crowd was absolutely quiet. He never imagined that such a huge number of people could be so quiet. Then Lucia jumped up. "Our Lady is coming!" she called. She was looking toward the east. Ti Marto looked too. At first he could see nothing but the blazing sun. But suddenly the glare grew less intense, and he could see a faint gray haze resting on the tree before which the three children were now kneeling. In the absolute stillness he began to hear a faint buzzing sound. One of those aimless thoughts that so often pass through people's heads at solemn moments came to him. That must be what it sounds like to talk on a telephone!

Then he heard Lucia say, "What do you want of me?" He looked at her closely, startled by the change that had come over her plain face.

The girl was radiant with the joy of love restored. What made her happiness even greater was the fact that the Lady apparently had not been offended by Lucia's doubts. She was looking down as serenely, as tenderly as ever. She said, "I want you to come back here on the thirteenth of next month. Continue to say the Rosary every day . . . to obtain the peace of the world and the end of the war."

Lucia was struck by a startling idea. She had no hesitation in putting it before the Lady. "People won't believe that you really appear to us", she added. "Would you do a miracle so that everyone will be certain of it?"

"You must come here every month on the same day,

and at the same time", the Lady said. "And in October I will perform a miracle so that everyone can believe!"

Lucia did not allow this dazzling thought to interfere with her many messages. There were several conversions. There was the crippled son of Maria Carreira. There was a very sick woman from Atougia who wanted to go to heaven as quickly as possible.

"Tell her not to be in a hurry!" the Lady answered. "Tell her I know very well when to come and get her!" Then she said, "Make sacrifices for sinners. Say often, especially while making a sacrifice: 'O Jesus, this is for love of thee, for the conversion of sinners, and in reparation for sins committed against the Immaculate Heart of Mary.?"

Again the Lady opened her beautiful hands, which twice before had literally poured the grace of God into their souls. This time she had another message for them. The people around the children saw the happiness on their faces fade and then give way to undiluted terror. Lucia gave a sharp cry. Her face was white.

The Lady was showing them a vision of hell—a vision made to fit their own understanding of the word. It was all there—the raging fire, the burning souls, the weirdly shaped devils, the cries of rage and despair. When the terrible picture disappeared, the Lady was still standing on the branch, looking sadder than the children had yet seen her.

"You have seen hell," she said, "where the souls of sinners go. It is to save them that God wants to establish in the world devotion to my Immaculate Heart. If you do what I tell you, many souls will be saved, and there will be peace. This war will end, but if men do not refrain from offending God, another and more terrible war will begin in the reign of Pius XI. When you see a night that is lit by a strange and unknown light, you will know that it is the sign God gives you that he is about to punish the world with war and with hunger, and by the persecution of the Church and the Holy Father.

"To prevent this, I shall come again to ask that Russia be consecrated to my Immaculate Heart, and I shall ask that on the first Saturday of every month Communions of reparation be made in atonement for the sins of the world. If my wishes are fulfilled, Russia will be converted, and there will be peace. If not, then Russia will spread her errors throughout the world, bringing new wars and persecution of the Church. The good will be martyred, and the Holy Father will have much to suffer. Certain nations will be annihilated. But in the end my Immaculate Heart will triumph! The Holy Father will consecrate Russia to me, and the world will enjoy a period of peace. In Portugal the Faith will always be preserved!"

There was one more secret. Until recently, no one knew what it was—except Lucia.

"Remember," the Lady said when she had finished this incredible message, "you must tell none of this to anyone except Francisco!"

Lucia's head was whirling. "Is there—is there any-thing else you want?" she asked faintly.

"No, my child. There is nothing more for today."

The Lady was hardly out of sight before the three children were surrounded.

"What happened?"

"What did she say?"

"What did she wear?"

"Why were you frightened?"

"What about my sick boy?"

"Why did you cry out?"

"I can't tell you!" Lucia cried. "It's a secret. A secret!"

Ti Marto swept Jacinta into his arms and looked around for a way of escape. A strange man tugged at his sleeve and shouted above the noise of the crowd, "Senhor—Senhor—can you get up to the road? I will get you home!"

Ti Marto elbowed his way out of the field, Jacinta on one arm, the other two clinging to his coat. Their unknown friend met them on the road. "Get in," he said, "and I'll get you away from here."

Poor Lucia and Jacinta and Francisco! They had just had such a tremendous experience that they paid no attention at all to what they were doing now.

Their first ride in an automobile! And they could not have cared less.

5

A QUESTION OF POLITICS

A SECRET!
Once the tantalizing word was out, the quiet, orderly life of the little village changed. Almost overnight it became a tourist attraction. Most of the tourists were wealthy people from the city. They planned a day's drive to Aljustrel as they planned outings to the zoo or the circus.

The main attraction to most of these odd people was not the idea that the children might actually have talked with the Mother of God. It was the secret that fascinated them. They were possessed of a witless, idle curiosity to know what it was, even if they did not believe the rest of the story at all.

People foolish enough to think like this in the first place naturally acted like perfect fools when they were face-to-face with their unwilling victims. "Do you like my bracelet?" a woman from Torres Novas purred at Jacinta one day. The little girl was trapped on her lap. "See? It has red stones and green stones. Isn't it pretty?"

"Yes", Jacinta said, wiggling.

The woman unclasped it and dangled it before the little girl's eyes. "Well, it's yours—if you'll tell me that secret!"

This sort of thing went on all the time. The children became experts at ducking the unwelcome guests who thought nothing of barging into their houses uninvited, even at mealtimes. One day while they were walking on the road to Fatima, they were stopped by a huge automobile filled with city people in picnic clothes. Before they could move a muscle to escape, one of the ladies had descended on them with a toothsome smile. "Can you tell us where the children who see our Lady live? We'd just love to talk to them!"

The three friends exchanged a quick look. "Certainly, Madam", Francisco said, politely removing his hat. "You just follow this road around the curve and down the hill.

The very first house as you enter the village is the Martos'." By the time the car had chugged away, the three were off the main road, over the wall, and running through the rocks and brambles of the wild hills where no Sunday tourist would ever find them.

Here they could talk and wonder over what the Lady had told them. How disappointed all the foolish people would be if they knew what the secret really was! The urgent need for the world to do penance would not seem very exciting.

And the fact that some place called Russia was a threat to the future? That would not have meant much more to the visitors than it did to the children. A few, more worldly wise than the others, might have known that Russia was a big country on the other side of Europe. They might also have heard that its weak-willed czar, Nicholas II, was being held prisoner by some revolutionaries. But why was it ever going to be a danger to the rest of the world? And what was all this talk about another war? Wasn't *this* supposed to be "the war to end wars"?

Of all the visitors, the three friends most dreaded priests. The sight of a cassock at the door was enough to send them scurrying for cover, even if it were only under the bed. But one day, as they were deep in conversation by the well, they heard the clip-clop of a donkey's hoofs on the cobblestone street. Before they realized what was happening, it was too late to do anything about it. They were trapped.

There was a priest riding the donkey. He climbed off

and came toward them. Lucia's face assumed the guarded, almost sullen, expression that she always showed to hostile grown-ups. But when the priest stood looking down at her, it relaxed into a radiant smile of joy.

"Do you remember me, Lucia?" asked the visitor.

She nodded eagerly.

"Will you take me to the place where our Lady stood?"

"Oh, yes, yes." Lucia seized his hand. "Do you believe us, Reverend Father?"

His eyes widened in surprise. "I believed in you four years ago, Lucia", he said. "Of course I still do."

It was Father Cruz, the saintly man who had heard her first confession.

When they had led him to the Cova and joyfully brought him to the Lady's tree, he said to Lucia, "You must love our Lord very much for all the graces he is giving you!"

During the fears and sorrows of the next few months, Lucia kept the glowing words close to her heart. For the second time, she felt, Father Cruz had arrived just when she needed him most.

As usual, the worst problems of these weeks were Lucia's. The ill will of her family had grown, and for a very good reason. Most of the Santos' farmland was in Cova da Iria. It was this area that was supposed to supply the family with most of its food for the coming year. But now the crops were ruined. Three thousand pairs of feet had trampled over them in one day. The steady stream of boots, sandals, and bare soles that had been stamping through them ever since had not helped!

Up to now, Antonio Santos had not had much to say about his daughter's strange behavior. He was a peaceful man. His easygoing ways led his more critical neighbors to the false belief that he was lazy. He went to Mass on Sunday, but he was by no means as interested in religion as his wife, so he dismissed all the fuss over Lucia as women's tales that would soon blow over.

But now things were different! His property was being destroyed by these women's tales. Weren't things bad enough as they were without looking for trouble, Antonio Santos wondered? When he was discouraged by the hardships of life on the Serra, he sometimes drank too much of the raw, heady wine of the district. At such times he expressed himself rather forcibly on the subject of Lucia's Lady and her terrible effect on his bean and potato crop.

Poor Lucia! She hardly dared to sit down at the table for meals anymore. "*You* can eat whatever you find growing in the Cova da Iria!" her sisters liked to snap at her as they divided the poor pickings among themselves.

"Yes", Maria Rosa grumbled as she added more water to the already thin soup. "Next time you see our Lady, ask *her* to feed you!" She laughed unpleasantly. "And while you're at it, why don't you ask her to do something to make people believe your stories? After all, the Blessed Virgin made a spring for Bernadette! Why can't she do as much for you?"

The other girls snickered.

"I've already asked her", Lucia said simply.

"And what did she say?" Her mother's voice was mocking.

"That in October she will do a miracle and make everyone believe she really came to us."

Her sisters let out shrieks of derision, but Maria Rosa said nothing at all. She was speechless.

The girl *was* mad after all.

While the family mourned the loss of its beans, a new kind of trouble was brewing outside the Serra da Aire. Had they known about it, none of their problems at home would have seemed very important.

News of the visions at Fatima had passed over the little mountains that enclosed their sheltered world. The shepherd children of Aljustrel had come to the attention of the government, which took an extremely dim view of them.

The new government of Portugal was violently anti-Catholic. In 1910—seven years before the first apparition—a bloody revolution had brought it to power. During its first few months in power, this government was so busy issuing decrees against the Church that it must have had little time to transact any other business. Religious orders were abolished, the Jesuits were exiled, the wearing of the religious habit was made a criminal offense, Catholic schools were closed, marriage was declared a civil contract, and of course Church property was confiscated.

Within a few years, one high government official predicted, no Portuguese boy would ever think of studying for the priesthood. The new minister of justice was even more hopeful. Within two generations, he wrote, Catholicism would cease to exist in Portugal.

But a strong and unified Catholicism had existed in Portugal for eight hundred years. And for all of those centuries the people had carried in their hearts a deep, unconquerable love for the Mother of God. It was to her that the Portuguese Catholics turned in their distress. In 1916 the Church arose to begin a new fight with an old weapon. All over Portugal a Rosary Crusade began. By the tens of thousands the Catholics of the country gathered every day to say the Rosary in their churches and homes and to receive Communion every Sunday for the salvation of their country.

The Rosary Crusade took the new "enlightened" government by unpleasant surprise. The Church was supposed to be dying! How had this resistance movement started in the first place?

This was the state of affairs in Portugal when, on July 23, 1917, the Fatima story first broke into print. A news item appeared in the Lisbon *O Seculo*, a violently anti-Catholic paper. Interviewing an "eyewitness" of the July apparition, the reporter described how the children (he thought there were only two) had fallen into an epileptic fit after seeing "a pretty doll with a halo". His own explanation of the business was this: someone with an eye for a fast dollar must have found a hidden spring on the property. Obviously they planned to transform the Cova da Iria into a second Lourdes and then go into the hotel business! The religious sideshow now going on was for publicity purposes.

"The authorities already know of the affair," the reporter ended, "and if they still ignore it, this will serve as a warning!"

Senhor Artur Oliveira Santos always read the Lisbon papers as soon as they arrived on the northbound train. Senhor Santos was the mayor of Villa Nova de Ourem, capital of the political district in which Fatima is located. Therefore, anything that went on around Fatima was the business of Senhor Santos.

The last line of the story made Senhor Santos furious. The authorities had no intention of ignoring the affair. The authorities did not need the unasked advice of a newspaper reporter on how to run the district, thank you.

Artur Oliveira Santos, not so long ago, had been a tinker. Now, at the age of thirty, he was mayor of the town council. And on the way up to this position he had passed a whole crew of lawyers, doctors, and professors who would gladly have been mayor in his place. People who looked down their noses at the political boss of the district and called him the "tinsmith" were not giving him his due. He was a shrewd, hard-working man. And he was devoted heart and soul to all the beliefs of the new government—including those on the "evils of religion".

"Hidden spring! Resort hotel!" Senhor Santos muttered to himself, stirring his coffee violently. "Anyone with a brain in his head should know that this is all some sort of plot hatched by the clergy!"

The mayor opened the file on the case, which he had already started to keep. Maybe they could get away with this in *some* places! But not in Fatima! "Nobody is going to make a fool of me in my own district!" he said out loud as he studied the calendar on his desk. The "pretty doll with a halo" had said she would be back on August 13. This was July 24. He would bide his time just a little longer, the mayor thought. He could afford to wait because, once he moved, he would move quickly!

"*Ai*, she is ruining us!" Maria Rosa's stolid face was distorted with rage as she shook the grim-looking letter under her daughter's nose. "All my life I have lived in this village and never have I had anything but 'Good morning!' from the police. And now! To be summoned by the law for disturbing the peace!"

Antonio Santos and Manuel Marto had been officially summoned to appear before the mayor on Saturday, August 11, at noon, and to bring their public nuisance children with them.

"Now!" Maria Rosa rumbled on, "you who tell lies to your own mother and your own pastor! Go tell them to the Senhor Mayor and see what happens to you!"

The name of Artur Santos (who was no relation to Lucia's family) was well known and cordially hated back in the hill country. Lucia grew pale. She looked help-lessly from her mother to her father, but poor Antonio was beyond words.

Early next morning father and daughter took a gloomy leave of the gloomy household and set out for Ourem. When they stopped by to pick up the other disturbers of the peace, they found Ti Marto eating his breakfast.

"Aren't you ready?" Lucia's father asked nervously. "We don't dare be late. Where are the children? Are they ready?"

Ti Marto placidly finished his piece of bread. He stood up. "No. But I am."

"Aren't Francisco and Jacinta coming with us?" Lucia asked.

"Now, Lucia, how can I take those two little ones all that distance? They don't know how to ride a donkey, and they certainly can't walk. Besides, I don't want them frightened by that—that man. I'll answer for them myself!"

None of these thoughts seemed to have bothered her own parents, Lucia thought sadly, as she rushed into the bedroom to find her cousins.

"Oh, Lucia!" Jacinta's smooth eyebrows were beetling with indignation. "Father won't let us go! But you've got to promise us one thing!"

"What is it, Jacinta?" Lucia asked, trying not to cry.

"If those bad men say they're going to kill you, then be sure to tell them that Francisco and I say exactly the same thing as you do!"

The interview with His Honor, the mayor, was, as it turned out, less trying than the hot, dirty ride into town. Lucia's father, terrified at the thought of being late, kept the donkey going at such a clip that Lucia fell off his back three times. When she actually stood in the awesome presence of Senhor Artur Oliveira Santos, the poor girl was too tired to care. She noted that the mayor was, after all, a very ordinary-looking man. She could hardly tell him from the newspapermen with whom he had carefully surrounded himself for this meeting.

Fifteen minutes later His Honor, the mayor, was wiping his forehead on a large handkerchief and fuming with annoyance while reporters scribbled in their notebooks and snickered softly. First, the Marto man had kept him asking questions for nearly five minutes before the mayor had finally caught on that there were three children involved, not two. Then the impudent fellow had looked him in the eye and told him that he had not brought these children along because they were too young! And then, the girl—the sullen and stupid-looking child who should have broken down after three minutes of questions! There stood the girl, her black eyebrows drawn together in a frown as big as her face, refusing to tell him a thing!

His Honor did not like to be defied by a ten-year-old girl. In exasperation he turned to her father. "How can you let this go on?" he asked. "Do you people in Fatima believe all this stuff?"

Under the fierce eyes of the mayor, poor Antonio

shuffled his feet. "No, sir!" he assured the mayor. "We believe it is a lot of women's talk!"

"I'm here too, sir," Ti Marto said calmly, "and I believe it—everything my children say!"

The mayor turned to the reporters and smiled as though he were saying, "You see the kind of people I have to do business with?" He turned back to Lucia. "Will you tell me this secret or not?" he bellowed. She shook her head. The mayor dropped to one knee so that his eyes were on a level with Lucia's. "Then take warning, little girl!" He shook his finger under her squarely set jaw. "You *will* tell me your secret, or you will die!"

This dramatic and quite false announcement would have been more effective if he had not had to release Lucia right after making it. Still, it had produced an effect on her. He could see that. She had turned pale, although she said nothing.

"Get out, now", the mayor said. "We'll meet again", he added, glowering at her. "I won't deprive myself of such charming company!"

The reporters laughed at this, and Lucia rushed out of the room as fast as she could go, followed by her father. Ti Marto looked thoughtfully at the mayor. "If you send for us, sir," he said quietly, "I know we'll have to come. But please remember that we have our own lives to lead." The reporters stopped laughing and put away their notebooks. The interview was over. Ti Marto had had the last word.

Artur Oliveira Santos was annoyed but not at all discouraged. The interview had turned out badly, perhaps, but he regarded it as only the opening move in the game. Now he would get down to the serious playing.

Ti Marto was out working on his farm when one of his many children came running across the field calling, "Father! Father! Come home—quick!"

It was about ten o'clock on the morning of August 13. Ti Marto had gone out to the farm partly because he had work to do and partly because he wanted to get away from the crowds of people that had been gathering outside and inside his house since dawn. He sighed wearily and trudged back home.

Tia Olimpia was sitting in the kitchen. She looked as though she had just seen a very unpleasant ghost. "What's the matter with you?" Ti Marto asked, as he washed the earth from his hands. She pointed in the direction of the living room, too upset to say a single word. Still drying his hands on the towel, her husband went in and looked around.

His Honor, the mayor of Villa Nova de Ourem, was sitting in the center of Ti Marto's parlor, puffing a thin cigar.

"I did not expect to see you here, sir", Ti Marto said coolly.

The mayor stood up and flashed a dazzling smile at his host. "I thought that, after all, it would be better to see the miracle today myself. Let's all go together in my carriage!" Ti Marto looked at the mayor suspiciously.

He obviously had something in mind, but Ti Marto did not know what. "You see, I'm like Saint Thomas", the mayor added hastily. "Seeing is believing!"

Ti Marto said nothing.

"Well, well," said the mayor, rubbing his hands briskly, "where are the children? Isn't it time to leave for the Cova?"

"There's no need to invite them", Ti Marto said. "They know when it's time to go!"

At that moment the three came into the room, looking for Ti Marto. When Lucia saw the mayor, she gasped and started to back out the door. "Wait!" he said, blocking the exit. "I'm going to drive you to the Cova in my carriage!"

"We'd rather walk", Lucia said sharply.

"But—uh—I'd like to visit Father Ferreira before we go to see the Lady. I told him I'd bring you to see him. And you haven't time to walk to Fatima first."

Lucia looked at her uncle. He shrugged and nodded, as if to say, "What can we do?"

By the time the carriage had reached Father Ferreira's house, the mayor had already used up his small supply of good manners. "Send Lucia in", he bellowed, after talking briefly with the pastor. Lucia marched up the stairs and into the priest's house. If the mayor wanted to play his question-and-no-answer game again, let him. Nothing could make her afraid today, knowing that in one hour she would be in the presence of our Lady.

As soon as she entered the room, Father Ferreira said wearily, "Who taught you to say the things you are saying?"

"The Lady I see in the Cova da Iria", Lucia replied promptly.

"Don't you know that people who spread such lies as you are spreading will go to hell? More and more people are being fooled by you. Look at the numbers who go to the Cova on account of you!" The presence of the mayor made him nervous.

Lucia said, "If people who lie go to hell, then I shall not go there because I am telling the truth! People visit the Cova da Iria because they want to. *We* do not tell them to go."

"Oh, come now", said the mayor abruptly. "Let's go!" Lucia looked at him in surprise. This interview with the pastor had been his idea. Now he seemed to have very little interest in it. He kept looking out the window nervously. "These are supernatural things", he added pointlessly as he hurried Lucia out the door and down to the steps where Jacinta and Francisco were waiting.

The two fathers were standing a short distance from the mayor's carriage, deep in conversation. Before either of them realized what was happening, the mayor came bursting out of the house, herded the three children into the carriage, and raced down the street in a swirl of pebbles and dust.

"Wh-at . . . ?" began Lucia's father. "Where . . . ?"

"He must be taking them to the Cova", said Ti Marto.

He looked up at the sky. "It is nearly time. We'd better hurry to meet them."

"Well, why didn't he wait for us?" grumbled Antonio.

But neither the children nor the mayor were among the several thousand people whom the two men found gathered at the Cova. Twelve o'clock came and still the children did not arrive. The crowd was getting restless. Rumors were spreading. The murmur of voices had begun to build to an ominous roar when a flash of lightning suddenly streaked across the sky. Instantly the crowd was silent.

Before the startled eyes of Ti Marto and others who were standing near the azinheira, a little cloud, white and delicate, appeared over the tree. It hovered there for a moment, then rose into the air and disappeared.

Ti Marto's heart sank. There was no doubt in his mind that the Lady had come all the way from heaven to keep her appointment. But where were the children?

"Ti Marto! Ti Marto!" A neighbor pushed his way through the crowd and came running up to him. "The mayor has kidnapped your children! I passed his carriage on the road, driving like the wind toward Ourem!"

Tia Olimpia, when she heard the terrible news, cried as though her heart would break. Her little lambs in the power of that evil man! And Jacinta—so timid and shy that she could hardly speak to strangers even in her own home! What would Jacinta do now?

But Maria Rosa took the news more calmly. "What are you fussing for, Olimpia?" she asked her weeping relative. "If they are lying, this will teach them a good lesson! And if they are not lying . . ." She stopped, struck by this strange idea for the first time. She shrugged helplessly. "If they are not lying, then our Lady will take care of them!"

6

A SENTENCE OF DEATH

W HEN THE MAYOR'S HORSE turned onto the main
road and started racing in the direction of
Ourem, Lucia said suspiciously, "This isn't the way to
the Cova! You took the wrong turn."

The mayor muttered something about going to talk
with the priest at Ourem and then returning to the Cova

by automobile. But when they reached the town he drove directly to his own house and hurried the three children up to a room on the second floor.

"Now!" he said briskly, waving the key of the door under their noses, "now I think it's time to put an end to this game!"

Francisco started to protest, but the mayor held up his hand. "No, don't argue. You can think it over." He fitted the key into the outside lock. "You'll have plenty of time to think it over, too, because *here you stay* until you tell me that secret!" He left the room and slammed the door shut.

This was the first chance the three friends had had for a quiet talk since early morning. For a moment they just looked at each other. Then Francisco said, "What time do you suppose it is, Lucia?"

"It's past noon. I know it is!"

"Then we'll *never* be able to meet the Lady on time! Let's try the window!" But the window opened over a discouragingly long drop to a concrete porch. The little boy's face clouded. "She'll come to look for us and we won't be there! And then maybe she'll be angry and never come back again!"

"Oh, Francisco, don't be silly!" Jacinta had been thinking the situation over during the wild ride from Fatima. She had worked it all out to her own satisfaction. "On Saturday that man told Lucia he'd kill her if she wouldn't tell him the secret, didn't he? Well, we're not going to tell him, are we?"

"Of course not!" her brother said impatiently. What a silly question!

"Then he'll kill us," Jacinta said, "and we'll go straight to heaven and see the Lady there!"

There was one person in the house, besides the three friends, who had a large fund of common sense and a kind heart as well. The mayor's wife, Adelina, thought it was all nonsense. She lost no time in telling this to His Honor. "What a stupid thing you have done!" she said sharply as her husband came down the stairs. "The people will never stand for it. Why did you do this?"

"I was simply taking out insurance against another miracle in my district!" He laughed. "It's simple. No children. No miracle. The people standing around the Cova da Iria go home feeling foolish, and they don't come back again looking for more thrills. Besides, now that I've got them here, I'll get that secret out of them if it's the last thing I ever do!"

His wife rolled her eyes. "Ah! You and that secret! What is it you hope to get out of them? You think they are lying about seeing our Lady on top of a tree, don't you?"

"Since there is no such person as our Lady to see on a tree or anywhere else, I think they are lying, yes!" he snapped.

"Then why do you care if they tell you this secret?" the Senhora shouted. "Won't it just be another one of their lies?"

"Women!" muttered the mayor, reaching for his hat.

He clapped it onto his head. "Now try to get this through your mind", he said, stalking toward the front door. "Whoever is teaching these three little parrots what to say must have some long-range plan—some plot in mind to make my administration look foolish at the next election. That's all this secret will turn out to be, you'll see! It's just . . ." He struggled for the right word. "It's just dirty politics, that's what it is!"

And he stamped out of the house.

"Men!" the lady muttered after him, and marched up the stairs. She unlocked the door and said, "Come on, little dears. Let's go downstairs and play with my children." She gave them all the latest picture magazines to look at and fixed them a fine supper. It turned out to be a pleasant afternoon, for the mayor's children were not bad company. It was not, after all, their fault that their father had named them Democracy, Liberty, and Republic!

But in the morning, when the first excitement had worn off, Jacinta began to be sad. Her resolve to suffer martyrdom for the Lady was in no way changed. She was perfectly willing to die—and the sooner the better! But so long as she was still alive, she wanted her mother.

At ten o'clock in the morning the mayor sent for the children and flung a handful of shining coins on the table. "Tell me the secret and they're yours!" announced His Honor. The three willing martyrs simply looked at him. He changed his methods and began to fire questions at them, first together and then separately. But he could not catch them in a contradiction, and he could not trick them into letting out the secret.

At last he shrugged his shoulders and said, "Well, well—I've tried to be nice to you, but you won't let me." He opened the door. "Candido!" he called. "Come in here!"

A burly head appeared in the doorway.

"Take them to jail," said the mayor, "and you know what to do next!" He laughed a nasty laugh.

The principal cell of the town jail was a dark, reeking room where all of the town criminals were herded together. There was no distinction between murderers, pickpockets, drunkards, and harmless vagabonds. When the door opened and three small children were shoved in among them, the inmates were so surprised that for a moment they could do nothing but stare.

"All right," said the mayor's assistant pleasantly, "just make yourselves at home. You won't be here long—just until we get the cauldron of oil boiling!"

Francisco's eyes widened. One of the prisoners said, "The—what?"

"Oil", said the man. "Boiling oil." He directed his remarks to the children, who had taken refuge at the far end of the room. "The mayor has tried to be reasonable with these three, but there's nothing left to do now but throw them into boiling oil!" The door of the cell shut behind him with a dismal clang.

Now Lucia and Jacinta and Francisco were not very sophisticated young people. They knew very little of the ways of the world that lay outside the Serra da Aire. They had read no books. They had seen no movies. They had no idea what their legal rights were. Did the political boss of the district really have the power of life and death in his hands? They did not know.

The existence of sin—yes, this they knew. They understood the kind of evil that might make a man throw them into a pot of boiling oil. But the mean, cowardly kind of evil that would make him *pretend* to do such a thing—no; nothing in their brief dealings with life had prepared them for this kind of evil.

When the mayor's assistant announced that the oil was being heated, that, as far as the children were concerned, was that. In an hour they would join the company of martyrs.

Jacinta started to cry and was terribly ashamed of herself for doing so. She turned and looked out of the window to hide her tears. Lucia was not fooled. She put her arm around her cousin's shoulders and said, "Why are you crying, Jacinta?"

"I'm crying only because I'll die without seeing my mother and father. And because nobody even cares what happens to us!" the little girl sobbed.

Francisco squared his shoulders. The game was almost up, but he was determined to see it through with courage. He was very conscious of his duty during these last hours. Lucia might be the oldest, but he was the man! And Jacinta was his little sister. "Now, Jacinta", he said, patting her on the back. "It's awful not to see Mother and Father again, but it's just that much more to offer up for sinners. Come on, now, let's say our Lady's prayer."

Jacinta hastily dried her eyes. She had grown strong in the belief that anything she could offer for sinners was well worth suffering. The three friends knelt down on the dirty floor and said, "O my Jesus, this is for the love of you, for the conversion of sinners, and in reparation for sins committed against the Immaculate Heart of Mary."

"Now look, little folks . . ."

Jacinta looked around quickly and jumped up. Their fellow prisoners had crossed the room and were standing in a cluster behind her. For a moment the little girl was frightened by the sight of so many rough-looking faces. But one of the men said gently, "You shouldn't be in a place like this! You've got to get out of here! Tell that mayor what he wants to know and go home!"

"Oh, we couldn't do that", Lucia said, standing up. "Our Lady told us not to."

The men looked at each other, surprised. For a chance to be on the other side of that iron door, all of them would have told the mayor everything they knew.

"I've got it!" said a pickpocket. "If you don't want to tell him the real story, just make something up. Then you can get out of here and fool him, too!"

This seemed a splendid idea to his companions. They nodded with satisfaction.

Jacinta shook her head, her large eyes free of tears now. "Oh, no," she said politely, "you see, that would be a lie!"

"*Ai!*" the man muttered, clapping his hand to his forehead. "Who cares about telling a lie to that wretched mayor?"

"Aw, leave them alone!" another man said. "Look—I have a concertina. You like to dance?"

"Oh, yes!" Jacinta's eyes sparkled as the man began wheezing out a tarantella.

"May I have this dance, Senhorita?" The pickpocket bowed solemnly in front of her.

"Thank you, Senhor!" she agreed, returning his bow.

Although he bent himself almost double, the difference in height between himself and his partner was too much of a problem. Finally, he swooped her up in his arms and did all of the footwork himself. It was such a funny sight that Lucia and Francisco burst out laughing. The other prisoners began to sing and the children joined in happily.

But when the dance was over, Jacinta asked her partner to put her down. She whispered to Lucia, "We have only a little time left. I don't think we should spend it dancing. Here! Let's put this up on the wall." She had found a little medal of our Lady in her pocket, and she hung it on a broken nail.

The children knelt down and began to say the Rosary. Their fellow-prisoners knelt, too, and prayed with them, many for the first time in years. In the middle of the last mystery, the door burst open and two policemen came into the cell.

"We're ready now", the first one announced. "Come

on." Ignoring the furious remarks addressed to him by the good thieves, he herded the three children into another room. The mayor's assistant, Senhor Alho, was waiting.

"The oil is boiling famously now!" he said to the policeman. "Take *her* first and throw her in!" He pointed to Jacinta.

"Our Lady, help me!" the little girl called out as she was taken out between the two policemen.

"Don't be afraid, Jacinta! We will see you soon!" her brother called after her. He turned aside and began muttering something, his lips moving rapidly.

Senhor Alho moved in hopefully. "What's that you're saying, Sonny? You got something to tell me, huh?"

Francisco eyed him coolly. "I am saying a Hail Mary so that my little sister won't be afraid", he said with some dignity, and went on praying.

In a few minutes the policeman returned. "Your sister's cooked. Don't *you* be so stubborn. Come on, tell His Honor what he wants to know, or you're next!"

"I can't tell him", Francisco said simply.

"Then come on!"

"I'm coming. Good-bye, Lucia. Don't be afraid! I'll pray for you from heaven!"

"Good-bye, Francisco. I'm not afraid!"

But when she was alone, she prayed for courage. When the man came back she interrupted his cruel description of Francisco's death by saying, "Everything we said about the Lady is true, and I won't tell you her secret!"

The policeman shrugged. "Then let's not delay. Come on!" As they crossed the hall, he added confidentially, "The oil is *really* sizzling now!" He flung open the door of the execution chamber and pushed Lucia in. She closed her eyes tightly for a moment. Then she took a deep breath and opened them, determined to look death boldly in the face.

What she saw was not a cauldron of boiling oil but the two shining faces of Jacinta and Francisco and the faintly purple face of His Honor, the mayor of Villa Nova de Ourem. He was saying, "You're going home, but don't think that just because you've escaped this time, you can go on acting this way. Next time, let me tell you, I won't be so lenient with you, and *then . . .*" The voice droned on and on, but the children did not hear it.

Their souls were flooded with joy, with the grace that is reserved for a very special few. They had accepted martyrdom as surely and as freely as Saint Peter, or Saint Agnes, or Saint Joan had accepted it. That they happened to be alive still was a matter entirely beyond their control.

As for His Honor, the mayor, who can blame him for uttering a lot of nonsense at the end of the scene? He had played the last card in his hand and had lost the game. He did not like losing to three children so stupid that they would choose to die over an imaginary Lady who stood around on the top of a tree!

7

A DELAYED MEETING

N<small>EXT MORNING</small> the mayor ordered his horse hitched up, and he drove the three prisoners back to the exact spot from which he had taken them—the steps of Father Ferreira's house in Fatima.

It was August 15, the feast of the Assumption. Just as the children were hastily clambering from the mayor's carriage, the last Mass of the day ended, and the parishioners began to pour out of the church. Ti Marto was among them. Suddenly he heard someone shouting at him, "Hey, Ti Marto! Look! It's your children! On the porch of the rectory!"

Ti Marto covered the square in about three steps, swept Jacinta into one arm, and hugged Lucia and Francisco with the other. Tears of joy streamed down his face. The entire congregation was pouring across the square cheering, and shouting, and muttering. Jacinta had been mistaken in thinking that no one at home cared anything about their fate. It had been the seething resentment of the citizens of Fatima that had finally made Artur Santos bring the children home. But the mere fact that they were home, and apparently unharmed, did not make the people any happier about their mayor. As the children came out of the rectory, followed by His Honor, a group of village boys began picking up sticks and stones in a way that worried the peace-loving Ti Marto.

The mayor said to him, "Come and have a drink with me, Marto?"

Ti Marto refused, then immediately changed his mind. He had better stay by the side of the wretched, bungling man, he thought, until the temper of the crowd had cooled. "I'll have a drink with you", he said, and guided the mayor safely through the angry people and into a tavern. As he was going in, Jacinta tugged on his sleeve and whispered something in his ear. He nodded and kissed her again. The three children scurried away.

"You may be sure I treated the children very well, Marto", lied the mayor when his wine had been poured.

"I'm not the one who's worried", Ti Marto said. "It's the people who want to know. This affair *could* have turned out very badly, as you probably realize!"

"Where are the children, by the way?" asked the mayor, anxious to change the direction of the conversation.

Ti Marto smiled an unhappy smile. "On their way to the Cova da Iria. Unfortunately, they are about forty-eight hours late for their appointment."

Three days passed. On Sunday, the nineteenth of August, Lucia took the sheep out to graze in the cool of the late afternoon. Francisco and his older brother, John, went with her, but Jacinta had gone to visit her godmother.

Near the village there was a little field called Valinhos. It was a peaceful place, surrounded by a rocky wall and shaded by olive trees. Here Lucia pastured the sheep and then sat down on a flat rock to rest. The children were quiet. Francisco stretched out on the cool grass, his hands locked behind his head, thinking. The boy felt, without putting it into exact words, that he had grown up more than six days' worth between the thirteenth and the nineteenth of August.

Only one thing now frightened him. They had not kept their appointment with the Lady in the Cova da Iria. Her carefully made plans had been upset by the meddling of a rash human being. If she simply had decided to give up the whole idea, after such an insult, Francisco thought sadly, who could blame her? This was the idea that had haunted him since his return.

But this afternoon he felt happy. Both the shepherds and the sheep were enjoying the cool greenness of Valinhos. Lucia, singing softly to herself, began picking a bouquet of wild flowers. All at once she looked up at the sun and blinked. It was only four o'clock, but the light had softened markedly. A fresh breeze had sprung up, and although there was not a cloud in the sky, a flash of lightning zigzagged over the field.

Francisco leaped to his feet and exchanged a quick look with Lucia. Was it possible?

Lucia turned to her cousin. "Please, John, run quickly and get Jacinta! Our Lady is coming!"

The boy stuck out his chin stubbornly. "No, I'm not leaving! I want to see our Lady, too!"

"*Please*, John! Jacinta has to be here! Wait a minute . . ." Lucia dug into her pocket and pulled out a few small coins, her entire worldly fortune. "Here—take this—and I'll find some more for you somewhere! I promise! But hurry!"

John grabbed the money and ran toward home. He dashed into the house, hollering "Jacinta!" at the top of his lungs.

"What's the matter with you, boy?" his mother asked.

"Lucia wants Jacinta at Valinhos right away, Mother!" he said, panting.

"Ah, that Lucia!" Tia Olimpia shook her head sadly.

"That Lucia! Does she think she is a priest that she always has to have her altar boy with her?"

"But Mother, Lucia says our Lady is coming and that Jacinta just *has* to go!"

Olimpia looked into the boy's earnest face and said, "Then go with God, my boy. Jacinta is at her god-mother's house."

John raced down the street, and in a few minutes Jacinta was running toward Valinhos as fast as her short little legs could carry her.

But the Lady had no intention of appearing until the littlest of her three friends was present. As soon as Jacinta arrived, there was a second flash of light that seemed to pass directly over a little oak tree very much like the one in the Cova. For a split second Francisco closed his eyes, afraid even now to hope that it could be true. When he opened them again, she was there, looking down on them with such love that he felt as though he would burst with the force of the love he returned. For reasons we shall never know, he still could not hear what the Lady said. But today the look on her face was as clear as any words could have been. It said, "I know what you have done for me since the last time we met!"

Lucia murmured her usual greeting: "What is it that you want of me?"

"Come again to the Cova da Iria on the thirteenth of next month, my child, and say the Rosary every day!"

"And you *will* do a miracle so everyone will know we are not lying?"

"I will", the Lady promised again. "In October, I will perform a miracle so that everyone can believe. Saint Joseph will come with the Holy Child to bring peace to the world. And our Lord will come to bless the people. . . ."

Our Lord! And Saint Joseph with the Holy Child! And in October, only two months off?

Then Lucia remembered that a number of sick people had asked to be called to the Lady's attention. "Some I will cure during the year", the Lady answered. Her face, always serious, grew a shade sadder. "Pray", she said. "Pray very much! Make sacrifices for sinners. So many souls go to hell because no one is willing to make sacrifices for them!"

When she had said this, she arose from the tree and glided away into the east.

Jacinta and Francisco broke off the top branches of the tree and then raced home as fast as they could. The first person they saw was Lucia's mother. She was standing outside her house, chatting with some neighbors. Jacinta, her little face beaming with happiness, tugged at Maria Rosa's skirt and said, "Oh, Aunt! We saw our Lady today at Valinhos! She *did* come back!"

Maria Rosa's face hardened. "Ah, Jacinta," she said, "when will these lies end? Do you have to see our Lady all over creation now, every place you go?"

"What's all the noise about?" Lucia's father stuck his head out of the door, scowling. On Sunday afternoon he liked to take a nap in peace.

"Look, Uncle!" Jacinta held up the branch. "This is where our Lady stood."

"Let me see that!" Antonio took it from her hand. He held it close to his face and then held it under his wife's nose. "What's that?" he asked, puzzled.

Maria Rosa sniffed the branch doubtfully and shook her head. "I don't know", she said.

She could not possibly have known. Never in her whole life had she smelled any perfume like the exquisite fragrance that poured from the branch.

Lucia had been left behind with the sheep. When she reached the house, one of the neighbors said in a shrill, self-righteous voice, "So, Lucia! At it again, are you? And this time in Valinhos! If you were *my* girl . . ."

"Quiet, woman!" Antonio Santos rarely spoke in a voice of real authority. The woman blinked. So did Lucia. Her father still held in his hand the branch touched with the fragrance of heaven. "Now leave her alone, all of you!" He looked his wife straight in the eye and muttered, "You too!" As he turned back into the house he said, more to himself than to the others, "For what she says might be true after all."

8

A NEW FRIEND

As the date of the September appointment approached, there was not a town or village in Portugal where arguments over Fatima were not boiling.

How did all this affect the three children? Not in the slightest.

They could not read the papers. They had no interest at all in what people thought about them. They were interested in only one thing—in doing exactly what the Lady wanted them to do.

Alone together in the fields, they went over their four conversations with her again and again. What, exactly, had the Lady come to tell them? The secret that had everyone in such an uproar? Well, that too, of course, but the secret did not really concern them just now because they couldn't do anything about it.

There *was* a part of the Lady's message, though, that they could do something about immediately—today and every day thereafter.

"Make sacrifices for sinners!" They could still hear the sadness in the Lady's voice as she had said these words. *"So many souls go to hell because no one is willing to make sacrifices for them!"*

To help sinners get into heaven! This was what the Lady wanted them to do.

Lucia and Jacinta and Francisco were not people of great imagination. They did not look for hidden meanings in the Lady's words. "Make sacrifices", she had said. To them this meant only two things—doing something you don't like to do; not doing something you *do* like to do. Like drinking cold water in the cruel heat of the summer days. . . .

Out in the pasture one afternoon the sun was so hot and the air so dusty that Lucia began to worry about her little cousins. They were clearly suffering agonies of thirst. "I'm going to the nearest house and get some water," she said sternly, "and you two are going to drink it."

But when she came back with an earthenware pitcher

full of clear, sparkling well water and held it out to them, Francisco said, "I don't want any! It's *my* thirst and I'm offering it for sinners."

"Me, too", Jacinta said firmly.

"Oh, Jacinta, please take it! You know you need it!"

"But Lucia, I really don't want any!"

Lucia sighed and went over to a big rock with a hollow in the middle. Here she poured out the lovely, cool water for the grateful sheep and then returned the pitcher.

But how, they wondered, do you make sacrifices by doing something you *don't* want to do?

One day, while they were walking along the road to the Cova da Iria, Lucia tripped over something on the ground. It was a long piece of thickly wound rope. She picked it up and twirled it idly around her arm. Its scratchy surface was irritating, and she was about to throw it away when she had a startling idea.

"Look!" She held the rope out to Jacinta and Francisco. "If we made cords of this and wore them around our waists, wouldn't that be a sacrifice?"

The other two leaped at the idea. From then on they wore these horrible, scratching, itching, burning objects tied tightly around their waists all day and, for the time being, all night. This is such an unpleasant idea that we must remind ourselves of an important fact about these three—they were not, in any sense of the word, morbid. They were perfectly normal, down-to-earth young people. Rightly or wrongly, they did what they did for a practical reason—they wanted to make sacrifices for sinners, and this was a sacrifice.

In the minds of all three, but in the mind of Jacinta most of all, the thought of sinners in need of help had grown to be the most important thing in life. Jacinta, the little girl who, five months before, had gone home in a huff if a game of "buttons" went against her!

On the morning of September 13, such crowds as the little village had never seen began to pour into Aljustrel. The villagers were simply amazed that all these out-of-towners should travel all the way to the Cova da Iria to watch three children talk to a tree!

The people of the region were not being mean or spiteful about all this. They were kind, goodhearted people, but they were natural-born skeptics where visions and miracles were concerned. They were poor and uneducated, but they were neither ignorant nor superstitious.

We must not confuse their attitude toward the visions with a lack of religion. They were deeply religious people, and they had a warm devotion to the Mother of God. But the idea that this august Lady should ever take it into her head to come to a stupid little village like Aljustrel and talk to three of the neighbors' children—! This simply did not fit in with their ideas of what was proper and fitting behavior for the Mother of God.

By noon of the thirteenth, more than thirty thousand people jammed the roads to the Cova. The children themselves had a difficult time getting through the crowd. By the time they reached the spot, poor Lucia's head was whirling with the list of ailments, conversions, job requests, financial difficulties, and family quarrels that she was supposed to discuss with the Lady.

The children knelt down and began to say the Rosary. The powerful responses of thirty thousand voices answered them.

Suddenly Lucia stopped praying and jumped up. She had seen the lightning in the east. In a few seconds the Lady was standing before them.

Lucia murmured her standard greeting: "What do you want of me?"

The Lady said, "Continue to say the Rosary, my children. Say it every day so that the war may end. . . . Next time Saint Joseph will also come to you, with the Holy Child. . . ." The Lady inclined her head to look more closely into the radiant faces of her friends. In the loving tone of a mother whose children are doing something foolish in an effort to please her, she said, "God is pleased with your sacrifices, but you must *not* wear the cords of rope to bed at night!"

Lucia said, "I have so many petitions for you, from so many people . . ." She tried as hard as she could to keep everything straight in her mind, but it was hard to remember when her heart was nearly bursting with joy. "There is a little girl who is deaf and mute. . . ."

"She will grow better within the year", the Lady promised.

Lucia asked about some other cures and conversions.

Then she timidly mentioned the weary problem that had brought such sorrow to them. "So many people say that we are cheats and liars and should even be burned alive. . . ."

"But in October I shall perform a miracle," the Lady promised her for the third time, "so that everyone may believe!"

That was all. Lucia called to the people, "Look—she is going—look there!" And she pointed into the eastern sky until the Lady disappeared from sight. Again the children were shoved and pushed and pulled by the crowd until Ti Marto rescued them. But the crowd that had gathered for the September apparition differed in one important particular from the previous crowds.

This one had priests in it. One of them was there on a semiofficial errand. His name was Don Manuel Formigão. He was one of the country's leading scholars and theologians. No man in Portugal was better suited for the job of making the first real investigation of the apparitions in the Cova da Iria.

We must remember that the Church had not yet spoken a single official word on the matter. The Church never rushes in either to condemn or to approve the sort of thing that was happening in Fatima. She simply waits for a time in silence. The passing of time alone will usually take care of the false miracle and the faked vision. And, of course, a miracle or vision that is truly the work of heaven will not be in the least affected just because the Church ignores it for a while.

But if, after a reasonable time, people's faith in it seems to be growing rather than dying, then the Church will begin to investigate—slowly!

This is the way the Church works even under the best of circumstances. The bishops of Portugal had more than the usual reasons for moving carefully. They were already having desperate trouble with the government. If the Fatima affair turned out to be a hoax—as most people believed that it would—well, it was better not even to think about the scandal that would follow.

But now—Father Formigão was investigating.

"What do you think about it?" he asked some of the priests immediately after the September apparition.

"I think our Lady was here", replied his old friend, Monsignor Quaresma, a reliable matter-of-fact man who ran the business affairs of the Diocese of Leiria. Father Formigão was impressed. The monsignor and his companions had distinctly seen a globe of light hover over the azinheira and then rise into the east.

Two weeks later, Father Formigão went back to Aljustrel and knocked at the door of the Santos' house. He introduced himself to Maria Rosa and said, "May I please speak with your daughter and her little cousins?"

Maria Rosa curtsied and waved him into the house. She had to be polite to priests, but her heart was not in it! It was on the tip of her tongue to tell the reverend gentleman that her daughter had spent so much time being talked to by priests since September 13 that she had not done a full day's work! But instead, she sent a neighbor's boy over to the field where Lucia was gathering grapes.

On the way the boy met Jacinta and Francisco. Jacinta wailed, "Oh, not another priest! Francisco, do we *have* to go? They mix me up so!"

The boy frowned, then broke into a radiant smile. "I know! We'll go talk to the priest—and offer it up for some really bad sinner!"

"Oh, that's a good idea! Come on!"

Jacinta was shy in the beginning, but she collected herself in time to note with horror that Francisco had forgotten to remove his hat in the presence of the visitor. She threw him a broad signal, which he did not catch.

Don Formigão had been talking with the two Martos for about half an hour when Lucia arrived, carrying her basket of grapes with her. She was downhearted at the prospect of more talk, but she sat down at once and began to answer the questions that the priest asked in his serious, but friendly, way.

An hour later Father Formigão said good-bye and left the house. Then he went home and sat down and thought—about everything he had seen and heard since September 13. The priest made up his mind.

The children were telling the truth. He was convinced of it. At that moment the earthly affairs of the three friends took a turn for the better. They had found a friend. How good a friend they themselves did not yet know.

"Lucia," the priest said, "are you afraid?"

He had gone back to Aljustrel on October 11. He had found Lucia helping a stonemason repair a leak in the roof, but she had scrambled down the ladder to meet him. "Afraid of what, Reverend Father?"

"Of what might happen—of what people might do—if nothing occurs two days from now when your miracle is supposed to take place?"

Lucia's eyes widened in surprise. "But, Reverend Father, our Lady *said* it would happen, so it will!"

As they went into the house, Father Formigão said a silent prayer that the girl's faith would be rewarded. He himself did not look forward to October 13 with such stoic calm!

October 13! All over the country people were waiting for October 13, some in hope, some in fear, and some in absolute delight—delight that the fireworks at Fatima were finally going to blow themselves out!

While the children waited and prayed in joyful preparation for their next meeting with the Lady, preparations of another sort were being made in Lisbon, a hundred miles away. In the editorial offices of *O Seculo*, the largest Lisbon paper, three men were busy arranging something that had never before been arranged: newspaper coverage of a miracle!

They were among the delighted ones. "The brains behind the Fatima children have climbed out on a limb and sawed it off", said the publisher of the paper, happily puffing on a fat cigar.

"And *O Seculo*", said the assistant editor, "will be right under the tree waiting to catch them when they fall!"

The publisher smiled, pleased at the idea. "But this proves something to me, after all. When all this started, I would have bet my last shirt that someone in Rome was behind it—probably a Jesuit! Or, at least, the local bishops. But I must have been wrong. They're all much too clever to promise a miracle for a certain day and a certain hour when they know perfectly well they can't produce!"

The assistant editor shrugged. "That's true—but I still wouldn't bet they didn't start it all. What I think is that the kids have simply gotten out of hand. At first they recited their lessons like good children, the way the priests or the parents taught them. But then they began to get a sense of power—branch out a bit—add a few frills. You know how kids are. They love attention. And can you think of a better way to get attention than to promise the whole country that the Virgin Mary is going to perform a miracle for you on October 13?" He chuckled. "If you ask me, Holy Mother Church has got herself a bull by the tail and doesn't know how to let go. Serves her right for starting this hoax in the first place. What do you think, Avelino?"

He turned to the third man in the room, Senhor Avelino da Almeida, the editor of the paper, and Lisbon's leading reporter on national affairs. He was a freethinker of no religious belief. He was cynical, but he was honest. Once, he had been in the seminary, studying for the priesthood. But that was many years ago.

"I don't think it matters who started it. What does matter is that in two days it will all be over. I want to be sure that the people who were taken in by the story will at least think twice before they swallow this sort of thing again! Here's the way to handle it. On October 12—that's tomorrow—I'm going to use the front page for a background story: everything that has happened from the first vision right up to date, right up to the minute I leave for the train."

The assistant editor smiled. "Good. And end the article by saying good-bye to your readers. Tell them you're off on the morning train and that the next time they hear from you, you personally will have covered a miracle for *O Seculo!*"

"Is the photographer all set?"

"All set. He'll meet you at the train. I told him to give us plenty of good action shots of the crowd before and after—particularly if there's any violence when the miracle fails to come off."

Senhor Almeida stood up. "I'll give this story to the city desk by noon and then get a timetable." A shadow passed over his face. "I don't mind the first half of the trip," he said, "but when I think of that bus ride from Torres Novas, I think I'll apply for a raise! Otherwise . . ." he smiled slowly. "Otherwise, I'm rather looking forward to the thirteenth of October!"

9

A SIGN FROM HEAVEN

EXCEPT FOR LUCIA herself, no one in the Santos
household shared the reporter's enthusiasm. They
looked forward to October 13 with horror. The luckless
Maria Rosa had examined her conscience and her
memory many times over since May 13. "But what have
I ever done—what could I possibly have done—to de-
serve this in my old age?" Maria Rosa was in such a

frenzy that she believed as gospel truth every witless threat made by any self-important "prophet" of the village. "Do you know what they say?" she asked Lucia. "That if this miracle does not happen, our house will be bombed!"

On the day before the scheduled miracle, gloom brooded over the Santos household. Maria Rosa woke Lucia at dawn and announced that they had better go to confession at once since their hours on earth were so few! The weather that ushered in October 13 did not improve her mood.

All night long a damp wind had blown threatening gusts of rain into the faces of the thousands of pilgrims already gathered in the Cova da Iria. The sky over Fatima was banked with black storm clouds that had been drifting together since dawn. Soon a cold, driving rain was pouring in torrents over the thousands upon thousands more who were jamming every road and path to the Cova da Iria. From the Atlantic Ocean to the borders of Spain, the people of Portugal were coming to Fatima. The number has never been definitely known, but the generally accepted figure is seventy thousand.

Some came in cars and some in wagons. But most of them came on foot—old people and young people, poor people and not-so-poor people, mothers and fathers with infants in their arms, city people, country people, farmers and fishermen, office workers, and factory workers.

"With a sure step and cadence they stride along the dusty road, between pine and olive tree. . . . The sheets of water, driven by a heavy wind, strike the faces, turn the road into a pool, soak to the bone the travelers who are unprovided with hats. . . . But no one grows impatient or ceases to move on."

To whom do we owe this eyewitness report of the road to Fatima? To Avelino da Almeida, who had missed his bus connection and who had to walk the last lap of the journey with the other pilgrims! He was wet, and he was weary, but he was a good enough newspaperman to know that he was seeing a human interest story such as he would never see again!

As the morning dragged on, Lucia stood by the window, watching the steady procession of pilgrims march down the road. It was time for her to go now. As she wrapped her shawl around her thin shoulders, she felt her mother's hand close around her wrist. "Lucia . . ." Her mother's voice was different. It sounded almost tender. "For the last time, be certain of what you say or this is the end of us!"

"Don't be afraid, Mother. Nothing bad can happen to us!"

Maria Rosa seized her shawl. "I'm going too", she said unexpectedly. "If you die, then I'll die with you!"

Lucia stared at her mother in amazement. But suddenly her heart began to sing with a new kind of joy. Her mother really did love her after all! It was only fear that had made her so unkind. Only Lucia had not understood until now. She hugged her mother tightly; then she hurried out of the house with her and over to the Martos' home. Things were not going too well there, either. The house was swarming with muddy-footed pilgrims, and her Aunt Olimpia was almost at her wit's end.

"Get your dirty boots off my bedspread!" she was shouting at one of the uninvited guests, who had climbed onto the bed for a better view.

A priest had been trying to frighten Jacinta and Francisco, but he had not succeeded. Now a neighbor was trying to frighten Ti Marto. "You must not go today, Ti Marto! People won't hurt your children, no matter what happens, because they are so little. But *you*—it might be another matter!"

Ti Marto felt a hand tugging at his sleeve. It was Jacinta, her face smooth and completely undisturbed by the confusion all around. "Let's not worry about anything, Father", she whispered into his ear. "If we get killed, then we'll all go to heaven together!"

They went out into the blinding rain and began the slow, tedious journey through the crowds and through the mud to the Cova da Iria. The number of people they found there frightened Jacinta. A tall, brawny chauffeur swung the little girl up to his shoulders, forced his way through the crowds, and delivered her safely at the foot of the azinheira. Francisco and Ti Marto followed on foot as best they could. Maria Rosa, determined to play out her new role of heroic mother, clung grimly to Lucia's hand until they, too, ended safely at the center of the Cova. Behind them came poor Antonio Santos. He did not know what else to do, so he followed his wife.

A priest was standing near the children. He went up to Lucia and said coldly (perhaps because he had been out in the rain all night), "What time will our Lady appear?"

"At noon, Reverend Father."

The priest looked at his watch. "It's noon already!" he snapped. "I suppose our Lady is a liar!"

Lucia said nothing. Her head was whirling with excitement, and she could not collect her thoughts. She glanced anxiously into the eastern sky and saw nothing but more rain clouds. In a few minutes the suspicious and thoroughly chilled priest said, "Look at the time, you people! It's way past noon! Can't you see this is all nonsense? Go home! Go home!"

Nobody moved. Almost weeping, Lucia said, "Our Lady *said* she would appear, and she will!"

The suspicious priest had forgotten one thing. A government regulation had put the country on a new time system so that the time at home would be the same as the time at the battle front. But the children, who had no watches, of course, had always judged the time of the Lady's appearances by the height of the sun. What was noon to them was not noon to the priest's watch.

The angry man drifted into the crowd. The children simply waited. Their pretty dresses, specially made for the day by a pious lady of the region, hung like sodden potato sacks around their legs. The crowd waited, too. At the top of the hill two different kinds of reporters were ready, their notebooks in their pockets: Avelino da Almeida and Don Manuel Formigão.

At noon—or at 1:37 P.M. by all properly running watches present—Lucia suddenly gasped with joy. "Jacinta—I see the lightning now! Kneel down! Our Lady is coming!"

The three friends knelt in the mud beside the wilted flowers and the soggy ribbons with which Maria Carreira had tried to adorn the poor little azinheira, worn to a mere stump by the hands of the curious and the faithful.

The Lady stood looking down at them.

For the last time Lucia said, "What do you want of me?"

The Lady said, "I want a chapel built here in my honor. I want you to say the Rosary every day. Soon the war will end, and the soldiers will return home."

"Will you tell me your name now?" Lucia asked.

"I am the Lady of the Rosary."

The girl lowered her eyes, blinded for a moment by the radiance of the Lady's face while she said these words. She recalled herself with difficulty. "I, I have all these petitions . . ." she stumbled. "Will you grant them all?"

"Some I shall grant. Others I must deny." The Lady leaned forward and looked lovingly from one face to another. She had only one more thing to say. Of all the messages and all the secrets, revealed and unrevealed, it was the most important. It was the reason she had come five times from heaven to earth.

"People must amend their lives and ask pardon for their sins! They must not offend our Lord any more, for he is already too much offended!"

"Is that all you have to ask?"

"There is nothing more."

The Lady rose gently off the branches, as she had done before, but this time she did not disappear into the east.

Lucia suddenly rose to her feet. "Look at the sun!" she called out in a loud voice, although she could not afterward remember calling it. "Look at the sun!"

The rain had stopped. The black storm clouds overhead had separated. The sun, glowing like a silver-tinged pearl, was spinning in the sky. At its right stood the Lady of the Rosary. Before the enchanted eyes of the three children, another figure appeared at its left. Saint Joseph, and with him the Child Jesus!

The Baby was about a year old. He was dressed, not in the pallid, off-white with gold-border smock that his statues in church so often wear, but in a little robe of bright red.

Saint Joseph made the sign of the cross over the unseeing crowd. Then the vision of the Holy Family faded away and was followed by a vision of our Lord—as a man this time. With him was our Lady, dressed in the somber black robes of the Mother of Sorrows. The third vision was for Lucia alone. Again she saw her Lady, this time wearing the traditional garb of Our Lady of Mount Carmel. Was it a fleeting sign for the future?

These indescribable visitors followed each other rapidly and then quickly disappeared. During the few minutes in which they passed before the privileged eyes of the three children, the motionless crowd in the Cova had been staring fascinated at the spinning silver disc overhead. When the last vision faded, the sun began to turn more quickly. As it spun faster and faster, bright shafts of brilliantly colored rays poured out over the earth—red, blue, green, violet, yellow—in a dazzling succession of light that was reflected on the grass and the trees and even in the faces of the people.

Suddenly, with a convulsive leap, the furiously spinning disc hurled itself in the direction of the terrified crowd. Down, down, down it plunged, dragging a trail of scarlet flame behind it. It seemed to be falling at an incredible speed, as though it could cover the ninety-three million miles that separated it from the earth in a matter of minutes.

The silent wonder of many in the crowd had turned to stark terror. It was a fearful moment—even for the cool-headed ones who forced themselves to be calm, to observe fully, to remember clearly. Shouts for help, cries, and prayers for mercy rose from the crowd. Many who had come for the sole purpose of seeing the fraud unmasked were now on their knees in the slimy mud, loudly confessing their belief. A priest who had come with a real, sincere anger in his heart at the dangerous "hoax" was doing the only thing he could think of. He was quietly reciting the Act of Contrition. How else should one greet the end of the world?

After what seemed an eternity, and was, in fact, only a few minutes, it ended as abruptly as it had begun. The sun, no farther away, it seemed, than the lowest bank of clouds, stopped falling and quickly went back where it belonged. And there it hung in the clear patch of sky. It was motionless now, and a little paler than usual, as though the exercise of the last few minutes had tired it somewhat.

"The miracle! There was a miracle!"

A cry of relief, of joy, of triumph even, swept over the crowd. People surged around the three children, listening while Lucia called out the Lady's urgent plea for repentance. Then the crowd quickly dispersed. Most of the pilgrims who had come great distances were eager to be on their way, to spread the joyful news to their own villages.

But to the weary Tia Olimpia it seemed as though at least three-quarters of the whole seventy thousand were jamming the road that led back to Aljustrel and trying to catch a glimpse of her children. She found it almost impossible to think clearly about what had just happened. When she looked back over the events of the past five months, her mind simply was overwhelmed by the weight of mystery—the visions, the messages, the secrets, and now the miracle! And her own little ones at the center of it all! Now, as she trudged along through the crowd, trying to keep her footing in the slippery mud, trying vainly to catch a glimpse of her husband and children, Tia Olimpia's mind took refuge in a most unmysterious thought.

"Now I have to go home and clean up the place!"

She groaned out loud. It would take a week at the very least, she thought. At the moment it was impossible to tell the inside of the house from the road outside! Even the beds were filthy. Tia Olimpia tried to keep her mind fixed on the fact that the Mother of God had just performed a miracle for the sake of her children. But she could not entirely banish the thought of her mud-caked kitchen floor.

At the door of her house she finally caught up with Ti Marto and Jacinta, whom he carried in his arms. The little girl seemed faint with weariness, and her mother had whisked her into the house and started the teakettle before she noticed anything peculiar about the place.

She looked around curiously, then turned to Ti Marto. "Who's been here while we were gone?"

"What do you mean?" Ti Marto asked, distractedly. He was trying as politely as he could to close the door on some curious, but strange, faces. The house was already filled with relatives and friends.

"Well, look around a little!" Tia Olimpia exclaimed.

Ti Marto looked. He blinked and looked again. "But this is impossible!" he muttered after a brief tour of inspection.

From one end to the other, the house was clean, spotlessly clean, sparkling and fresh, as though the fall housecleaning had been finished five minutes before. Not a trace of the morning's mud was left. Not a single print of a single boot was on any of the floors or beds. The bedspreads looked as though they had been freshly washed, starched, and ironed.

"Who cleaned up this place?" Ti Marto asked, looking from one admiring face to the other. "Teresa? Was it you?" He turned to the children's godmother.

"Of course not! I was in the Cova all morning."

"Victoria? . . . Maria? . . . Gloria?"

The ladies simply looked at him. They had seen the place—before and after. They knew perfectly well that no one of them could have put it into its present shape in the length of time the family had been away. Not with all that dirt!

Ti Marto ran his finger over the kitchen floor. He had heard about floors being so clean you could eat off them. He had not expected it to be true of the mud-flat he had left a few hours before. He looked at his wife and shrugged. "Well," he said, "our Lady can do big miracles for the children and little miracles for the parents."

Tia Olimpia did not say anything. She just sat down in her rocking chair and sighed a great sigh of relief. She was exhausted by the emotions of the day. Besides that, her feet hurt. She had good reason to be pleased with the Queen of Heaven for remembering that she had once been the Queen of Housekeepers.

"It remains for those who are competent to speak out on the *danse macabre* of the sun, which today in Fatima has caused hosannas to burst forth from the breasts of the faithful and has naturally impressed . . . freethinkers and others without interest in religious matters who have come to this now-famous heath."

Senhor Avelino da Almeida pulled the last page of his story out of the typewriter and sent it down to the composing room. "Now," he thought grimly, "all hell will break loose!"

And of course it did.

Senhor Almeida had "covered" the miracle and written an honest story, as a good reporter should. He had kept his own reactions out of it as much as possible and concentrated on the reactions of the crowd. It was a historic piece of journalism. But, as he had predicted, it made people furious, particularly other newspaper people.

It would have been so easy for them to brush off the dance of the sun at Fatima as a case of pure mass hysteria. The people wanted a miracle, so they saw a miracle. What more natural explanation could anyone ask for? But how could they explain the fact that the cynical unbeliever, Almeida, had seen the same thing happen? Almeida, the observant newspaper man who had gone to Fatima for the sole purpose of reporting that the miracle had not come off as scheduled!

Many people in newspaper and government circles got around this by hinting that Almeida himself was, for some mysterious reason, in on the plot to deceive the people. After all, they recalled darkly, he *was* an ex-seminarian!

But more important opinions were being formed on the startling events of October 13. Thoughtful men—like Father Formigão and the others who would one day be called upon to study the case in the name of the Church—what did *they* think?

There were only three possible answers to what had happened that day in the Cova da Iria. Perhaps the crowd really had been suffering from hallucinations—as some newspapers insisted. Perhaps even the cautious Don Formigão and the cynical Senhor Almeida and other unbelievers and skeptics in the crowd had been hypnotized for a moment. How, then, did one explain the fact that the peculiar behavior of the sun was seen within a radius of fifteen miles by a great number of very surprised people who had had no interest at all in going over to Fatima for the day?

Or perhaps the miracle had been simply a natural phenomenon—a startling combination of eclipse, aurora borealis, and rainbow? This explanation satisfied many people, even though they knew that not one observatory in Europe had reported anything the least bit unusual in the behavior of the sun on October 13, 1917. But they had to admit that if this *was* a natural phenomenon of some sort, it was also a very strange coincidence. It just happened to occur in the very spot, on the very day, at the very hour for which three ignorant children had, for three months, been promising a sign from heaven!

What explanation was left?

The miracle had happened. Exactly how it happened is not too important. Had the sun really moved that day over Fatima? Or had the people been allowed to see a miraculous *appearance* of the sun falling toward them? Probably the latter, but who can say for sure? God, who created the solar system out of nothing, can certainly do what he likes with it.

Today—nearly a century later—it is easy to say that nothing much happened that day in the mountains of Portugal. But many people do say it, and many of them are priests. (We must remember that there is, of course, no obligation to believe that anything supernatural happened that day or any other day in the Cova da Iria.) And there are people to whom the quite frankly theatrical miracle makes no spiritual appeal at all. It would not be telling the whole story to pass over this without mentioning it.

But let us keep one fact in mind. Lucia did not ask for a miracle to convince the world a century later. She did not ask for a sign to appeal to sophisticated American Catholics. She wanted a miracle to convince her own neighbors—the tough-minded, unimaginative, you-have-to-*show*-me people who lived in the Serra da Aire. These were the people for whom the miracle was designed. These were our Lady's people, and she knew them well enough to know that no subtle sign would do! So she decided to hit them over the head with the sun. Can anyone suggest a better way of making the point?

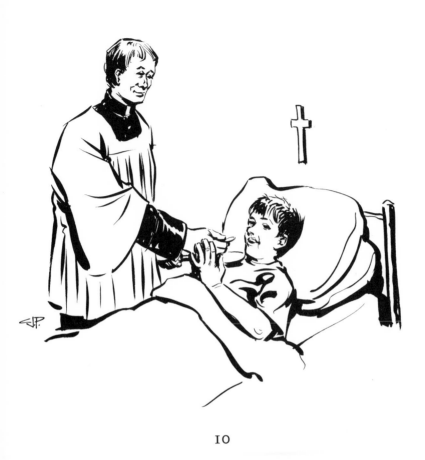

10

A PROMISE FOR FRANCISCO

I N THE WHOLE of Portugal no one resented the events
of October 13 so much as some of the men who
lived in the surrounding towns. The pro-government
freethinkers took the whole thing as a personal insult.
These country people from Fatima, they declared, were
giving the district a bad name! Something would have

117

to be done to prove to the snobs down in Lisbon that
not *all* the people up north were ignorant, superstitious
peasants!

A week after the day of the miracle, a handpicked
group from the Masonic Lodge at Santarem drove to the
Cova da Iria in the middle of the night and made off with
everything that could be moved. The table, the lanterns,
the candles, the little archway, and the other decorations
that the faithful Maria Carreira had put there—they
were all piled into the back seat of the car. But the prize
trophy was the azinheira, which they chopped down
with the ax newly sharpened for the purpose.

The next day these objects were carried through the
streets of Santarem in a mock-religious procession, to
the accompaniment of two large drums and the chanting
of a jeering, blasphemous "litany". The place of honor
was reserved for the azinheira. "Come one, come all,
and see the tree on which the Virgin Mary perched!"
chanted the marchers between guffaws, blissfully un-
aware that the last laugh was on them. They had chopped
down the most prominent azinheira in the Cova, but it
was the wrong one. Our Lady's tree had been worn to
such a humble little stump that they had paid it not the
least attention.

Other pilgrims were coming to the Cova da Iria. Even
before one stone had been brought in to begin work on
the Lady's chapel, the place itself had become a shrine.
From all over the country people came to pray in the
barren field. There was really nothing to see in it but

rocks and trampled vegetables and a little stump of a tree. There was nothing within miles that even faintly resembled travel accommodations. And now that the apparitions were over, there was no hope of seeing anything exciting or unusual happen.

But there was an irresistible aura of peace and holiness and pure devotion about the place that the pilgrims felt very strongly. One cold, rainy December day, Maria Carreira found an old man, his clothes soaking wet, kneeling by the tree. He had been praying there all night. "Are you all right?" she asked, running up to him.

"Oh, yes," he answered, "I *am* all right. I've never passed such a wonderful night as this. I feel very happy in this place!"

So did everyone who came to pray in the Cova. So did Maria Carreira, whose life had taken on an entirely new purpose since June 13. It is true that she was having more than her share of trouble because people insisted on leaving money there. She had even managed to get into trouble with His Honor, the mayor, which, of course, was very easy to do. But she was happy.

"Don't worry, dear, sweet Lady", she would think to herself as she puttered around the Cova, pulling up weeds and replacing candles. "Don't worry! I know we are slow, but we will get that chapel built for you yet!"

And Lucia and Jacinta and Francisco?

What had been happening to *them* since the thirteenth of October?

When the first hectic days were over, life became a little more serene than it had been for the past five months. Lucia was freed from the abuse and distrust of her family. The best her sisters could do now was tease her whenever she tried to sing, or dance, or enjoy any of the pleasant little pastimes she loved. "What? The girl who saw our Lady doing a thing like that?"

Lucia and Jacinta were going to school now. Maria Rosa did not understand what difference it made to our Lady whether Lucia could read or write, but what could she do?

Francisco, too, was still going to school. It was an awfully silly way to spend one's last days on earth, the boy thought. What good would it do him in heaven to know the multiplication tables or the length of the river Tagus?

Francisco was cheerfully unconcerned about his future. He simply took it for granted. What, after all, was life on earth but a means of traveling to heaven? If he was going to make the trip without any detours along the road, so much the better. The Lady had said she would come soon for him and Jacinta, so that was that.

On their way to school the three friends were often followed down the street by people who had urgent petitions for our Lady. Francisco took everyone's problems very much to heart. He would often spend the entire school day in church, kneeling motionless before the altar, faithfully working on the petitions put before him. It was a novel reason for playing hooky.

Francisco would pray his heart out for the consolation of anyone who had troubles. But, as the year passed, the boy began thinking in a new way. He found that he was most interested in praying to console God himself for the grief brought to him by the sins of mankind. All Francisco knew about it was that he loved God very much. He did not know any long, theological terms for describing his love. He did not realize that, without any spiritual help from anyone on earth, he was becoming what theologians call a contemplative.

Jacinta, too, sometimes seemed to have a direct line of communication with heaven. One day her Aunt Victoria came from Fatima to Aljustrel in great distress. "Where's Lucia?" she asked Jacinta, whom she found at home. "I want to talk to her."

"I don't know, Aunt Victoria. I think she's out in the fields. What's the matter?"

It was clear that the lady regarded Jacinta as a pretty poor substitute for the older girl, but she told Jacinta her story and asked her to pass it on to Lucia. Her son had left home—had run away for good, she added, bursting into tears. He had taken every piece of money he could lay his hands on and had left a note saying that he would be far, far away by the time they missed him! She did not care a thing about the money, she said, drying her eyes, if only he would come home!

Jacinta felt very sorry for her aunt and prayed as hard as she could for the return of the missing boy.

A few days later Aunt Victoria was back in Aljustrel.

Her son was with her. "I wanted to tell you this story myself," he said to Jacinta, "and ask you how it happened."

This was his story. He had got as far as Torres Novas and there spent the last of the stolen money. He had gotten into a street fight and been arrested. His glorious adventure in running away from home seemed destined to end in a jail a couple of miles down the road! But on the way to the jail, he managed to escape. He ran as fast as he could until his lungs were ready to burst. He did not care where he was running—just so it was away! That night he found himself in the middle of a pine wood. Not a sign of life was to be seen. There was no road to follow, not even a path. He was hopelessly lost in the woods. The wind was rising, and the would-be world traveler was seized by a terrible, heart-shaking wish for home. If he ever saw it again, he vowed, falling on his knees and praying for the first time in months, his life of crime would be over forever!

All at once he realized that he was not alone in the woods any more. A girl was coming through the trees. As she drew nearer, he saw that it was his little cousin, Jacinta. What was she doing in that godforsaken spot, he asked her. But, without a word, she took his hand and led him through the woods and out to the main road. She pointed in the direction she wanted him to go and then slipped away into the darkness. All night long the boy followed the unknown road and, when daylight came, he found himself in a village he recognized. From there he quickly reached his home.

No prodigal son was ever welcomed with more joy. He had come with his mother to thank Jacinta for her help and to ask her how she had found him.

But Jacinta smiled her shy smile and slipped away from the excited group that had gathered to hear the story. Later, when Lucia found her in one of their much-needed hiding-places she said, "Well, Jacinta, what's the answer? Were you in those woods last night? And how did you ever get there?"

Jacinta shook her head. "Oh, Lucia, you know I wasn't there! I don't even know where that place is. All I know is that last night I prayed and prayed to our Lady to bring our cousin home, wherever he was, because I felt so sorry for Aunt Victoria!"

Francisco and Jacinta felt that there was only one real sorrow in their happy lives. They had not yet been allowed to make their First Communion. So, on the eve of First-Communion Sunday, Ti Marto took them to the prior of Fatima to be examined in the catechism. Jacinta kept her wits about her and passed the test easily. And Francisco—the confidant of angels? He was so nervous in the presence of the pastor of Fatima that he forgot the Creed and was told to wait another year! Father Ferreira was cautious to the end.

In October of that year, Francisco came down with influenza. It was 1918. The disease had swept across the world in the wake of the terrible war that was just ending. Soon the whole family was ill, except for Ti Marto, who was happily spared to take care of the others.

From the very beginning Francisco knew that his illness was our Lady's means of fulfilling her promise. When he began to get a little better, it worried him that his mother was building up her hopes, for he really did not expect to come out of it. The question was settled in his mind very definitely one day when Jacinta, weak with fever herself, came to his room to visit him.

The Lady came in, too. She slipped in as gently and quietly as a mother entering the room of a sick child. She said, "Don't worry, Francisco; I will come for you very soon and take you to heaven!"

His face, flushed with fever and pinched with weakness, broke into a radiant smile. Then he had really said all the Rosaries she had wanted him to say!

"And you, Jacinta . . ." The Lady's eyes rested thoughtfully on the face of the valiant girl. "You have made so many sacrifices for sinners. Would you like a chance to make still more sacrifices for them before I take you to heaven?"

Jacinta's big eyes glowed. Was she really going to talk to the Lady herself? "Oh, yes, yes!" she said, hardly able to believe that it was her own voice.

"Then you must go to two hospitals—but not to be cured. Your mother will take you, but then you must stay there all alone and wait for me to come and get you. Will you do all this—for the love of God and for the atonement of the sins of the world?"

"I will; of course I will!" Jacinta said joyfully.

The Lady smiled lovingly at the two children and then

slipped away as quietly as she had come. Francisco waited patiently for her return. Even when he rallied a little in January, he was not fooled, although he was delighted with the chance to make a last trip to the Cova da Iria. Finally, in March, he had a complete relapse.

Lucia came to visit him every day on her way home from school. "Lucia, shut the door—tight!" he said to her one afternoon. He raised himself on one elbow, wincing with pain as he did so.

"Are you suffering very much, Francisco?" Lucia asked.

"Yes—but, for our Lord and Lady, so it's all right. Look, Lucia, you'd better take this." He reached under the bedclothes and pulled out the piece of twisted rope that he had worn since the day Lucia had first found it on the road to Fatima, a year and a half before. "I can't keep it any more, Lucia, because I'm so afraid Mother might find it!" Not one single part of their heroic sacrifices had ever been suspected by their families or anyone else.

Lucia nodded. "I'll take it for you, Francisco."

He smiled a little. "But I can still make sacrifices, Lucia, even though I'm so weak. You should taste that green medicine Mother gives me! Is it awful! Trying not to make a face is really work!"

By the end of March Francisco knew that just a few days were left. He had only one piece of unfinished business with life. "Father," he said to Ti Marto, "I really do want to receive Communion before I die."

Ti Marto's heart contracted sharply. He had no doubt that Francisco meant—and knew—that his death was near. But he nodded and said calmly, "And you shall, Francisco. I'll go see about it right now."

In Fatima Ti Marto found, to his great relief, that Father Ferreira was out of town for the day. A visiting priest was on duty at the rectory. Even before Ti Marto had finished his story, the good man was hurrying out of the house with him and back up the road to Aljustrel.

Meanwhile, Francisco had sent out an urgent message for Lucia. She came running up the street to his house and hurried into his room. "What is it, Francisco?" she asked. "What's the matter?"

His face was radiant with joy. "Father went for a priest so I can go to Communion!"

"Oh, Francisco, how wonderful!"

"So I'll be going to confession soon, and that's very important! Now *think*, Lucia. I want you to *think*! And then go ask Jacinta . . ." He stopped, breathless with excitement.

"Yes, Francisco? What shall I think?"

"Can you remember seeing me commit any sins that I might have forgotten?"

Lucia looked into the wide, innocent eyes of the dying boy and nodded slowly. "I see. Well, I'll think, but . . . I don't know of any, Francisco. Unless—well, sometimes when your mother told you to stay home you used to run off and come out with me and the sheep. Maybe that was a sin."

Francisco nodded gravely. "Yes, of course it was. Now go ask Jacinta."

Jacinta, with the unfailing memory of a little sister, supplied the reminder that once, before the Lady's visits, Francisco had sneaked a penny from another boy's pocket.

These were about the worst of the sins that Francisco Marto had to confess on that day in April which was close to the last day of his life. In the morning the priest returned with Communion. Afterward, Francisco, whose joy had made him almost unconscious of the outside world, took part in a brief, but important, ceremony without having the least idea that he was doing so.

The Church always takes a special interest in the last hours of people who claim to have had visions, for it is their last chance either to confirm or to deny their stories.

The visiting priest said gently, "Francisco, did you see our Lady five times in the Cova da Iria and once in the field of Valinhos?"

"Yes, I did", Francisco said, smiling at the memory.

He died the next morning.

11

A JOURNEY FOR JACINTA

JACINTA was the only member of the family who did
not go to Francisco's funeral. By that time she herself
was very sick with pneumonia. The attack was followed
by a terrible case of pleurisy. With every breath she took,
racking pains went through her little chest. "I don't
really mind", she said to Lucia one day. "But please don't
tell Mother. I don't want her to worry about me. And
Lucia . . ." She glanced toward the door of the room and

lowered her voice still more. "You'll have to take this for me because I'm afraid Mother will find it."

Lucia nodded silently and slipped the second piece of rope into her pocket.

Jacinta's case was too much for the local doctor. When he saw that an abscess had formed outside of one of her lungs, he threw up his hands in despair. "There is nothing more that I can do for her. She will have to go to the hospital at Ourem."

Jacinta was not surprised. This, she knew, was the first of the two hospitals our Lady had told her about. She went to Ourem and stayed there for two months. But in those days there was no real treatment for the disease, and she did not improve.

In August she was brought back to Aljustrel. For the rest of the year she stayed at home, in constant pain from the open wound in her side, but happy to be among the people she loved. Shortly before Christmas of 1919 she said sadly one day, "Soon I have to go to a hospital in Lisbon."

Her parents were horrified by the idea. Lisbon! It seemed like the other end of the world to the people of the mountains. If Jacinta went to Lisbon, she would have to stay there all alone. Besides that, they wondered, what could the dreadfully expensive city hospital do that had not been tried at Ourem? The poor child must be delirious.

It was an old and faithful friend who, unknowingly, saw to it that the Lady's plan was carried out. Father

Formigão dropped in at the Marto house for an unexpected visit. With him was a doctor from Lisbon and his wife. They had asked the priest to drive over to Fatima with them in their new automobile. Father Formigão suggested that, since they were so near, they might as well drive over to Aljustrel and see how everyone was getting on. By this chance event the Lisbon doctor was brought to Jacinta.

He was shocked by the sight of her. So was Father Formigão. After examining the open wound in her side, the doctor called the priest and Ti Marto into the next room. "The wound is infected", he said. "It's impossible to take care of it here. She needs an operation."

After a few more whispered words, the three men went back to the girl's bedside. Ti Marto said, "Jacinta, Father Formigão and the good doctor, they—they think you need more . . ." He hesitated, hating with all his heart to put it into words. "We are going to send you to a fine hospital in Lisbon", he ended weakly.

She nodded. "Yes, I know", she said.

Ti Marto tried to smile reassuringly. "But only for a little while! Soon you'll be back home—all better!"

She smiled back at him and said nothing. She knew that she would never come home again.

Of all the sorrow that lay behind her and ahead of her, nothing seemed so bitter to Jacinta as the separation from Lucia. "We shall never see each other again", the little girl said, clinging to her beloved friend for a last moment. "Pray for me, Lucia; pray for me very much until I can go to heaven! And then I will pray, and pray, and pray for you!"

Lucia stood for a long time, silent and dry-eyed, looking after the cart that was taking Jacinta and her mother and brother to the station. She was beyond the point of tears. She thought, as she so often did, of what the Lady had said to them on the day of their first meeting. "You will have much to suffer, but the grace of God will be with you and strengthen you!"

She had never needed it more than she did at that moment.

Upon their arrival in Lisbon, the travelers were met by some city ladies who apparently thought it would be very edifying to befriend the miraculous seer of Fatima.

When they saw the exhausted, half-dead child, their enthusiasm cooled. The festering sore in her side was covered by her dress, but it was all too evident to anyone around her. This wasn't quite so uplifting as it had seemed in the beginning, the ladies decided. They had met the train, as agreed, but they suddenly had no idea at all where Jacinta could stay until her admission to the hospital had been arranged.

The sick girl and her mother and brother found themselves tramping the streets of the strange, frightening city, looking for someone to take them in. Soon they lost count of the number of institutions that had turned them away at the door. After hours of walking, they finally came to an orphanage run by a nun named Mother Godinho.

This nun had been following all the developments at Fatima with growing interest and devotion. She had thought many times, "If only I could go there and talk to the children!" Thus when Jacinta herself unexpectedly walked into her parlor, the good woman was almost speechless with surprise and delight.

Here, at last, the exhausted girl found a refuge, and here, after her mother had to leave her, she spent two happy weeks with the good nun and the twenty-five orphans in her care. The nun, whom Jacinta called her "little mother", wrote down as many of her conversations with the girl as she could remember. It seemed to her that the wisdom of this simple, uneducated, ten-year-old bordered on the supernatural.

"Who taught you all these things?" she asked the girl one day.

"Our Lady", Jacinta said. "But some I think of myself. I love to think."

There was a chapel in the orphanage. The joy of actually living in the same house with her "hidden Jesus" helped to relieve her homesickness. And once Ti Marto made the long, weary trip to Lisbon to spend an hour with her. He had to take the next train home because Tia Olimpia and several of the other children were very sick, and once again he was the only one able to take care of them.

When the time came, Mother Godinho took Jacinta

to the hospital for the operation that the Lisbon specialist wanted to try. Jacinta was so weak that the surgeons were afraid to give her anything but a light local anaesthetic. She suffered beyond description during the operation and during the next week, particularly when the incision in her side had to be dressed. But her patience seemed endless.

Mother Godinho came every day to the dark, cheerless hospital ward. One afternoon she found Jacinta, whom she had left the day before in great misery, sitting up in bed looking at a picture book. The girl's face was radiant.

"Jacinta!" the nun exclaimed. "What has happened to you?"

"Our Lady was here, Mother. She said she would come for me right away now! And she said that while I waited I wouldn't have any more pain!"

As Mother Godinho left the ward that evening, she met one of the hospital doctors. "Your little friend is doing very well today", he told her. "The operation was a complete success. I think she'll be leaving here soon."

"So do I, Doctor", murmured the nun. Her eyes were filled with tears both of joy and of sorrow.

On the evening of February 20, Jacinta sent for the parish priest who took care of the hospital patients. He heard her confession, and she begged him to bring her Communion at once. "At *this* hour, dear child? But you're not fasting. In the morning . . ."

"But Reverend Father, it's the Holy Viaticum I want, and you don't have to be fasting for that, do you?"

"No, but you can receive the Viaticum only when in danger of death, and you're much better. All the doctors say so, don't they?" He turned to the nurse who had just come on night duty.

"Oh, yes, Jacinta", she said. "You're getting better! The doctor is so pleased, and we're all so happy for you!"

"You see?" said the priest. "I'll bring you Communion in the morning."

But when he came back in the morning, Jacinta was dead.

She was buried in Ourem in the family vault of a young nobleman who had befriended the family. Here her body stayed for nearly fifteen years, until a new tomb was built in Fatima for her and Francisco. Then her body was brought home. The fourteen words inscribed on the stone tell the whole story:

"Here Lie the Mortal Remains of Francisco and Jacinta, to Whom Our Lady Appeared."

12

A NEW LIFE FOR LUCIA

LUCIA WAS ALONE now. Her companions in this heavenly adventure had carried out their part of the bargain. The rest of it was up to her. With all her loving heart, Lucia rejoiced at the present happiness of her two friends. But she missed them terribly. There was not one person left on earth to whom she could talk about the things closest to her heart. Lucia felt like a stranger in her own home. A new kind of invisible barrier had grown up between her and her family. They were kind to her, of course, but they were never really at ease with her any more.

In other ways too, it was a sad year for the family. Antonio Santos died suddenly a few months after the last apparition. Lucia grieved for her father, whom she had loved so much. Even while he was alive it had made her unhappy to hear the unkind, untrue things that the holier-than-thou gossips of the village said about him— that he was a drunkard and a wastrel and that he never went to church. She knew that these were lies. Now that he was dead, it hurt her even more to hear the cruel stories that grew in the telling, as all such stories do.

At the time of her husband's death, Maria Rosa herself was in poor condition. She had terrible attacks of asthma. The doctor was sure that her heart was affected. It was terrible to see the strong, forceful woman so weak that she could hardly lift her head from the pillow. Maria Rosa, the unconquerable! The tower of strength! The house, already saddened by the death of Antonio Santos, was filled with gloom.

One wet winter night, as Lucia sat by the hearth staring into the fire, her sister Maria said to her, "Listen, Lucia, Father is dead, and if Mother dies, we'll be orphans. If you really saw our Lady, why can't you ask her to make Mother better?"

Without a word Lucia got up and hurried out of the house. She ran through the rainy night to the Cova da Iria and fell on her knees before the holy place of the apparitions. "Please let Mother get better! My sisters and I will come here for nine days to thank you! And we'll feed nine poor children! And . . . and . . ." She tried to think of something to say that was in some way equal to her feelings. "And we'll come here on our knees from the road to the tree!" Then she gathered up a little of the earth from the base of the azinheira and carried it home.

"What kind of drink is this?" Maria Rosa asked suspiciously when the girls handed her a cup of tea with a little of this earth.

"It's just tea made of flowers", Gloria told her. "Drink it up. It will do you good."

Maria Rosa shrugged, as if to say that nothing could do that. But she drank it. Within a day or two it became clear that our Lady would not refuse the first really personal favor her friend had ever asked her. Maria Rosa's attacks of breathlessness stopped completely. Her heart grew stronger. Soon she was out of bed and working as usual. "It's very strange", she told her neighbors. "I thought I was just a sick old woman—and would be until the day I died! But I feel almost young again!"

When the girls went on their knees to the Cova, to fulfill the promise, they went at night so no one would see them. Maria Rosa walked after them to say her own prayers of thanksgiving. If this were a novel, we would see her walking there in triumphant faith, the last doubt gone forever from her mind. But people in real life are more complex than people in fiction. Did Maria Rosa Santos really believe, even then, that our Lady had appeared to her daughter with a message for the world? Not completely. She knew what she had seen on October 13, but what if her eyes had deceived her? She would never again accuse Lucia of lying. But why should the Mother of God have chosen so ordinary a girl, particularly one with so unworthy a mother? These were the humble doubts that remained in Maria Rosa's mind. In the village of Aljustrel the belief is still strong that when she died in 1942 a few doubts were still there.

Lucia realized that she now had all the responsibility for guarding the Lady's secrets and carrying out her wishes. She knew very well that the Lady would somehow arrange matters so that her orders could be carried out. But how?

Although Lucia had no way of knowing it, the first step had already been taken. The diocese of Leiria, to which Fatima belonged, had been without a bishop for many years. But in May 1920, the Holy Father appointed a new one. He was Don José Correia da Silva, a famous theologian from the seminary of Santarem, where Father Formigão also taught. He was a fair-minded man, but he was also a very prudent one.

The bishop realized that he had inherited more problems than those of reorganizing a diocese. Of all the men in Portugal, the good man thought grimly, why did *he* have to be the one to come to grips with the Fatima situation? It would be a long and complicated business, of that he was sure. But he knew exactly what the very first step had to be.

On the feast of Saint Anthony—just four years after that other festival to which Lucia would not go—Maria Rosa and her daughter answered the bishop's invitation to visit him in Leiria.

He took them into his study and closed the door. "I want to talk to you about your future, Lucia", he said. "But everything we say here must be kept a secret." He smiled a little. "You are good at keeping secrets, I am told."

Lucia blushed but said nothing.

"How are things going for you in Aljustrel?" he went on. "Do people still come to your house to get a look at you, and ask you questions, and ask you to pray for them?"

Lucia lowered her eyes. She did not think it would be dignified to tell the bishop that, because of the time she had to spend answering questions, she had no time to take care of her sheep! "Oh, yes, my lord", she said instead. "Almost every day someone comes to the house. And on the thirteenth . . ." She stopped, embarrassed to have to admit that she was such a center of attention.

"How would you like to go away from here, Lucia, to a very fine school where you can get a real education—and live in peace?"

Lucia's eyes widened. "Oh, yes!" she said eagerly, for peace was what her present life lacked.

"That way," the bishop went on, "you will be free of all these people who want to question you—and who might end up by confusing you about exactly what did happen in the Cova da Iria. Also, it will stop the tongues of those who say that the pilgrims come to Fatima only out of curiosity to see Lucia Santos." Since he was a courteous man, he did not add that, if this were really true, her departure would also stop the pilgrims from coming at all and settle the whole thing. "Is it agreed?"

"Oh, yes, my lord!"

"Good. You will go to the Dorothean Convent at Vilar. The mother superior has already agreed. But remember, Lucia, you must tell no one where you are going, or even that you are leaving the village. Not even your closest friends must know. And when you get to the school, you will tell no one who you are or where you come from. Is it agreed?"

"Yes, my lord."

"Good." He stood up and walked around the desk. "It is hard," he said, "but it is the best way. You'll see."

"Yes, my lord."

"There is one thing more." He looked down at her solemn face sympathetically. "You will not speak to anyone—to anyone at all—about the apparitions at Fatima. It must be as though the whole thing had never happened."

Lucia hesitated for a fraction of a second and then nodded her head.

There were no outward preparations of any kind for Lucia's departure. She had very little to pack, and she was not allowed to say good-bye to anyone. On her last day at home the neighbors saw her walking toward the Cova. They did not know that she was making a pilgrimage of her own.

She knelt in the tiny chapel that the dogged persistence of Maria Carreira had built there at last.

Lucia looked up at the statue that had been put there only a few days ago. It was a pretty statue, Lucia thought, smiling a little. The sculptor had consulted with her carefully about it. But it was as far from the beauty of the original as a candle is unlike the sun.

As she walked slowly out of the Cova da Iria, she wondered whether she would ever see the place again. She put the question out of her mind. The future was full of questions. She would not ask any of them. She would simply wait.

She had only one more mission to perform before she went home. In her pocket she carried the two cords that Francisco and Jacinta had given to her. She laid them in a hollow in the rock and set a match to them. In a few minutes the dry rope was in ashes. Lucia felt as though she had burned the past.

"Good heavens! What has his lordship wished on us?" the mother superior thought as she studied the stubborn-looking mountain girl, fresh from the grime of an all-night train ride. She said stiffly, "You understand that not a soul in the convent knows who you are—except myself and our reverend chaplain?"

Lucia nodded silently.

"When you are asked your name, say that it is Maria das Dores."

"Yes, Reverend Mother." Lucia felt that at the moment the name Maria of the Sorrows fitted her very well!

"And when anyone asks where you came from, tell them that you are from a village near Lisbon." Lucia nodded. "And of course you will not discuss the Fatima episode with anyone", the mother superior added. "Very well. Sister will take you to the dormitory now. Classes begin in an hour."

"Thank you, Reverend Mother."

As she was leaving the office, the nun called, "Maria das Dores!" Lucia continued to walk. "Maria das Dores!" the superior repeated sharply.

Lucia turned around quickly. "Oh, excuse me, Reverend Mother", she said, terribly flustered. "I—didn't—"

"I wanted to tell you to go downstairs for breakfast before going to class. Sister will show you the way."

"Thank you very . . ."

"And try to remember, my child," the nun interrupted, her chilly voice a shade warmer, "that a girl named Lucia Santos has simply ceased to exist."

For four years Lucia followed the bishop's orders to the letter. She led the ordinary life of a convent schoolgirl with all its ups and downs and satisfactions and irritations. She went to class when the others did and to chapel when the others did. She worked hard and became a passable student. She learned how to do a cross-stitch, how to pour tea, and how to conjugate irregular verbs. Gradually the rough edges of the Serra da Aire began to wear off. Lucia was growing up into a well-bred, well-liked, self-possessed young lady.

During all those years not one word did she speak of her former life—except to her mother, whose rare visits were so dear to her. And even to Maria Rosa she said not a word about the apparitions.

Only once did the convent itself have to take her true identity into account.

"Maria das Dores", the mother superior said to her one day after calling her into the office and closing the door. "As you know, your class is to take the state board examination next week."

Lucia frowned a little. "Yes, Reverend Mother. We're all studying very hard, and we hope . . ."

"There's only one difficulty, my dear. It is against the law for anyone to take this examination under an assumed name. Would you mind—would you be too disappointed—if you didn't take it?"

Lucia's plain face lit up with a smile of sheer delight. "Why—no, Reverend Mother", she said, trying hard not to burst into song. "I wouldn't be too disappointed!"

By the time Lucia was eighteen, she had decided about the future that was staring her in the face now that her school days were coming to an end. She had become an avid reader. One of her favorite books was the life of the Little Flower, Saint Thérèse of Lisieux, and it had helped her to make up her mind.

"I would like to become a Carmelite", she confided to the Mother Superior—a new and friendlier one.

"A Carmelite! Oh, my dear child!" the good woman exclaimed. "The cloistered life of the Carmelites is much too rigorous. I'm sure you're not strong enough. Do choose another order!"

Lucia thought about this for a while and then went back to the superior. "I would like to become a Dorothean sister, if you think I would be admitted", she said.

The superior beamed. "And why do you want to enter the religious life, Maria?" she asked.

"So I can go to the chapel more often", Lucia replied promptly.

"I—see." The superior was puzzled. This was hardly a standard reason for claiming a vocation to the religious life. "You are still very young for such a decision, dear. Wait a little."

Lucia agreed and did not say another word to the disappointed superior. The year passed. Then one day the mother general of the Dorotheans came to the school to talk to the graduating class. "What about the little Santos?" she asked the superior. "What are her plans for the future?"

The good lady threw up her hands. "Who knows what Maria das Dores is thinking about *anything*? Such a good, honest, jolly girl, and yet . . ." She shrugged help-lessly. "She is a puzzle. Once, she wanted to join our order, but she has changed her mind, I suppose."

The mother general sent for Lucia and said, "Maria das Dores, have you completely given up the idea of the religious life?"

Lucia blushed deeply. "Oh, Reverend Mother! I have never given it up for an instant!"

"But why have you said nothing about it all year?"

Lucia looked surprised. "But Reverend Mother—I was told to wait. So I waited."

Maria Rosa accepted the news with her usual stolid calm. She was lonely in her widowhood. The older girls were marrying, one by one, and her eldest son had gone to South America. She missed Lucia terribly, but she would not really have had her come back to Aljustrel to take up life where she had left off. The child belonged in the convent, her mother thought. What place was left for her in the world?

Lucia had been gone for five years, but she had not been forgotten. For some time now an old acquain-tance—a friend, in a sense, for he had shared an hour of triumph—had become very curious about her. Shortly after she entered the novitiate, Senhor Artur Santos, mayor of Villa Nova de Ourem, summoned her mother and said sharply, "What has become of your daughter? Where is she?"

There had been a time when a summons from the

mayor had made Maria Rosa frantic with fear. But she, too, had grown up a lot in the past five years. She looked the Honorable Santos straight in his honorable eyes and said, "My daughter is where she wants to be—and where *I* want her to be." With that, she marched out of his office.

The mayor muttered a few well-chosen words at her retreating back and then opened the file labeled "Cova da Iria". He did not like the way things were going there. There was practically nothing in life he disliked more.

13

A MISSION ACCOMPLISHED

LUCIA ENTERED the Dorothean convent of Tuy, a city just across the border of Spain. Here she settled into the routine of the novitiate with her usual good-natured zeal, and she was very happy. The same kind of easy leadership that had made her so popular with the children of Aljustrel made her a favorite among her fellow novices. How surprised they would have been to hear

the history of Maria das Dores, as they listened to the
wonderfully comic songs she sang to them during recreation or watched her busily nailing up scenery for the
Christmas pageant.

There was only one hidden sorrow in Lucia's life. The
ban that had been put on the subject of Fatima had
followed her into the convent. Not one word that per-
tained in any way to the apparitions was allowed to reach
her. It never occurred to the straightforward Lucia that
this silence was all carefully arranged. Since she had
heard nothing about it for seven years, she came to the
conclusion that our Lady's visits had been forgotten in
Fatima. It made her sad to think of the Cova da Iria as a
deserted field—a restored vegetable garden, probably—
with no one to remember or to care that the Mother of
God had once blessed it with her radiant presence.

Then one day a Jesuit priest came to visit the convent.
He knew that Lucia was there under an assumed name,
and he looked for an opportunity to speak with her. "I
want to tell you that I met your mother not long ago",
he said. "She's very well and she seems very happy."

"How kind you are, Reverend Father", Lucia said,
smiling. "But whatever took you to Aljustrel? Have you
friends there?"

"Oh, no. I was in Fatima for the May 13 pilgrimage,
so naturally I went to Aljustrel, hoping to meet your
family. I'm afraid your poor mother and sisters must get
awfully tired of pilgrims who want to meet them and—
what's the matter, Sister?"

The novice looked confused. "I don't understand you, Reverend Father. *What* May 13 pilgrimage were you in?"

"Why—the one to the Cova da Iria." He laughed uncertainly. "How many shrines do you think there are in the neighborhood of Fatima?"

"But—do you mean that people still go to the Cova da Iria to pray?"

The priest opened his mouth and closed it again. For a moment he looked as confused as the novice. Then he understood everything. "You don't know anything about it", he said, rather than asked. "Why not?"

"I don't know. No one has said anything to me about the Cova da Iria for years. The bishop said I was not to ask any questions about it, so I didn't."

For a moment the Jesuit could think of nothing to say. He had really put his foot into it this time, he thought. Or had he? Briefly he considered all the angles. The bishop's orders were seven years old. Perhaps he had simply forgotten to revoke them. Perhaps not. But in any case, it just wasn't fair. What harm could there be in the simple truth? And who had a better right to it than Lucia?

He reached into his pocket and pulled out a medal. "You've never seen one of these?"

Lucia shook her head. "What is it?"

"It's a medal of Our Lady of Fatima."

"*Our Lady of Fatima?*" she repeated in a whisper.

"And the good bishop who said you weren't to ask or

answer any questions? *He's* been asking the questions lately. You didn't know that a canonical inquiry has been set up to study the case?" Lucia shook her head. "Well, you would have heard about all this soon anyway, because eventually the committee will get around to asking *you* a few questions. I think the reason they haven't had to see you yet is that one of the priests on the committee has such a complete record of all his talks with you. As a matter of fact, he's already published two editions of a book about Our Lady of Fatima—and got himself into quite a little trouble with the authorities for doing it! A Father Manuel Formigão. Do you remember him?"

Suddenly Lucia could see herself as a child—downhearted because she had to talk to a priest—carrying a basket of grapes into the house. And Francisco was sitting there with his hat on. And Jacinta was so upset because he didn't remember to take it off. "I recall him", she said, her face expressionless.

"After the bishop ordered the commission to meet," the priest went on, "the pro-government freethinkers in the neighborhood were so put out that they planted five bombs in the little chapel and blew it to bits!"

"Oh—no! Poor Maria Carreira!" How strange it seemed to say the name again after so many years. "And the tree stump? Was it . . ?"

"No! Four bombs went off. The fifth one—the one right over the tree—was a dud! Well, after the bombing, people were so angry that they made the May 13 pilgrimage that year a tremendous one! Of course it was small compared to some of the numbers that have been there since! On this last May 13 there were about four hundred thousand people. And in July, the bishop himself was there for the first time. There are always crowds there on the thirteenth of May and in October, of course. But at other times, too."

He stood up and began to walk around the narrow parlor. "You see, Sister, there's a feeling about the place. I don't know how to describe it. Not only when there are big pilgrimages or a miracle, but . . ."

"Are there miracles there, too, Reverend Father?" she interrupted, trying to keep all traces of emotion out of her voice.

"Oh, yes, I've heard of many and, more important, I've seen a little girl who was totally paralyzed for a year get up and walk away. But—well, it's a funny thing about Fatima. The physical cures are wonderful, of course, and very exciting. But people seem to take them pretty much for granted. Naturally there are cures at such a place. It's the other kind of miracle—the kind that won't ever be certified by a medical board—that people feel most strongly."

He paused to rub his forehead with the fingers of his left hand. "How can I explain it? It's, well, Fatima is a rebirth of faith—of the individual and of the nation." He smiled. "Just how cut off from the world are you novices, anyway? Do you ever read the papers? Do you know what's been going on in Portugal lately?"

"We don't see the papers, but we certainly know that

the Church in Portugal is stronger and freer than it has been for years." She smiled a little to herself. "And, at recreation, we're informed of every new revolution."

"In that case recreation must be one constant current events class! But you don't know that Our Lady of Fatima—*your* Lady—is generally credited with the improvements—by people who approve of them and by people who don't approve of them? Oh, the anticlericals are furious at her!"

The priest sat down again, facing Lucia. "When I see the incredible awakening that Portugal has undergone at the Cova da Iria, I begin to think that Our Lady of Fatima doesn't mean to confine her efforts to one little country. I think she really has something to say to the whole world!"

The bell rang for vespers. Lucia stood up at once and held out her hand. The priest shook it in silence.

She said, half to herself, "I thought it would be like that", and hurried out of the room to answer the summons of the bell.

Lucia took her first vows as a Dorothean sister in 1928. She was very happy. So was Maria Rosa, who came from home for the ceremony, bringing the only gift Lucia would admit she wanted—a hive of the good Aljustrel bees to keep the community supplied with honey.

Lucia was Sister Maria das Dores now. She was an ideal member of the community—faithful to the rule, always cheerful, very devout, but without a trace of false, or long-faced, piety. Even as a dignified nun she never quite lost the quick wit and sense of fun that she had had as a girl. One day Lucia and another sister had been sent out shopping. They walked the short distance from the convent to the international bridge that begins in Spain and ends in Portugal.

Just as they crossed the bridge into Portugal a pair of elegantly dressed ladies stopped them and said, "Aren't you Dorothean sisters? Are you from the convent in Tuy?" The sisters nodded. "Well, we're just on our way there now. We've heard that Lucia, the seer of Fatima, is in Tuy and we do so want to see her! She *is* there, isn't she?"

There was a split second of silence. Then Lucia said, "No, ma'am. She's not in Tuy. She's back in Portugal now."

Lucia's companion was seized by a sudden fit of coughing and buried her face in a handkerchief. The lady said, "Oh, dear, I'm *so* disappointed. I wonder how we can find out where she is. If she *were* in the convent at Tuy, could we have seen her?"

"Why—certainly, ma'am", Lucia said.

"How would we go about it?"

"Why—just by looking at her, ma'am", Lucia said cheerfully. "Just as you're looking at me."

Yes, Lucia was a tourist attraction again, for the fame of Fatima was spreading. It made her happy to know that her Lady was being venerated in the holy place where she had appeared. But, strictly speaking, it was not her first concern with the Lady of Fatima.

Our Lady had never said to her, "You must make people come here by the hundreds of thousands to pay me honor!"

She had not said, "You must make the bishop approve of devotion to me."

But the Lady *had* given Lucia a commission to carry out!

"If you do what I tell you", she had said, "many souls will be saved and there will be peace. This war will end, but if men do not refrain from offending God, another and more terrible war will begin. . . . To prevent this I shall come again to ask that Russia be consecrated to my Immaculate Heart, and I shall ask that on the first Saturday of every month Communions of reparation be made in atonement for the sins of the world."

How impossible it had seemed at that time that Lucia Santos, the sheepherder from Aljustrel, would ever be able to carry out these orders! And many times during the next twenty-five years it seemed as impossible to Sister Maria das Dores as it had ever seemed to Lucia Santos!

To get the Lady's wishes carried out was a long, uphill struggle.

It began in 1925. While Lucia was alone, one day, in her room, our Lady appeared to her again as she had promised. She asked once more for the devotion of receiving Communion and reciting the Rosary on the first Saturday of the month. Lucia immediately told her superior and asked her help. The superior did not know what to say or do. She thought for a moment, then said, "I know! Write your old confessor in Vilar. Perhaps he can tell you what to do."

But the priest did not even answer the sister's letter. Her first timid efforts had got her exactly nowhere.

Lucia then turned to the men who had always seemed to be there with help in the crises of her life—the Jesuits. From then on it was always to Jesuit confessors, in Tuy and later back in Portugal, that she passed along the Lady's wishes. In 1929, the Lady appeared to her again as she knelt alone in the chapel. This time she made the most difficult request of all. She asked for the consecration of Russia to the Immaculate Heart to obtain peace for the world.

"This message might be more important to the world than even we can guess", Lucia's Jesuit confessor said. "Write it out exactly as our Lady said it, and I, myself, will see that it gets to Rome."

But in Rome the message was read, filed away for future reference—and forgotten. Rome is a busy place that must carry on business with the entire world. An urgent message from a Portuguese nun about another war, and the need to consecrate Russia to the Immaculate Heart of Mary? Well, it was all very interesting, but it didn't seem to have much to do with anything going on in 1930.

The years passed. Lucia had done all that she could

do—except pray for help. And then, on the night of January 25, 1938, she awoke to see a strange light pouring through the narrow window of her room. The sky was blazing with light—an eerie, blood-red glow that was seen all over Europe. Observatories said it was the most unusual aurora borealis in history.

But to Lucia the strange light in the heavens had another meaning. As she leaned her head against the windowpane and watched the crackling northern sky, she thought of the Lady's words: *And when you see a night that is lit by a strange and unknown light, you will know it is the sign God gives you that he is about to punish the world with war and hunger, and by the persecution of the Church and the Holy Father.*

Now surely there was no more time to lose! Lucia wrote at once to the Bishop of Leiria. She begged him to do something and to do it quickly. "Write to the Holy Father", she was told, and again she did.

But Pope Pius XI was very ill by the time Lucia's letter reached him.

The saintly Pope's last year was saddened by terrible signs of trouble ahead. In March of 1938—less than eight weeks after Lucia's flaming sign in the sky—a man named Adolf Hitler marched his army into the neighboring country of Austria and seized its government. After that, the future was all too clear.

Pope Pius XI died in February of 1939. The next month Cardinal Pacelli became Pope Pius XII. The cardinal had been made a bishop on May 13, 1917, at the hour in which our Lady had made her first appearance in the Cova da Iria.

By now it was clear that Europe was standing on the very brink of disaster. On March 14, two weeks after the new Pope's election, Czechoslovakia fell to Germany. In April, the Italian dictator, Mussolini, seized Albania. And, in September, German troops marched into Poland. The whole world would soon be plunged into war.

Lucia wrote to the bishop: "If the world only knew the moment of grace that is conceded to it, and would do penance!" And for the third time she wrote a letter to Rome.

At last, after years of trying, Lucia found someone ready to listen to her. The message that had seemed so unreal in 1929 was all too easy to understand in 1940.

After a careful study of the case, Pope Pius XII consecrated the entire world to the Immaculate Heart of Mary, with a special mention of the people of Russia. Ten years later he would fulfill the exact request of our Lady with a separate consecration of Russia.

"Just as not many years ago We consecrated the entire world to the Immaculate Heart of the Virgin Mother of God, so now, in a most special way, We dedicate and consecrate all peoples of Russia to that same Immaculate Heart, in confident assurance that through the most powerful protection of Mary there may at the earliest moment be happily realized the hopes and desires for . . . the attainment of true peace . . . and of rightful liberty for all."

So it was finally done. When Lucia read the Pope's words of consecration, she thought again of what the Lady had said so many years ago. "If my wishes are fulfilled, Russia will be converted and there will be peace; if not, then Russia will spread her errors throughout the world, bringing new wars and persecution of the Church. . . . But in the end my Immaculate Heart will triumph. The Holy Father will consecrate Russia to me, and she will be converted, and the world will enjoy a period of peace."

14

A PILGRIMAGE TO FATIMA

L UCIA DID SEE the Cova da Iria again.

It happened in 1946, four years after the Pope had consecrated the world to the Immaculate Heart of Mary. On May 20 she went back to Fatima for a short visit, accompanied by the mother provincial of the Doro- theans. Her arrival came at the end of an exciting week. On May 13 the triumphant Lady of Fatima had been crowned Queen of Portugal. Eight hundred thousand people were watching, including all the bishops of Portugal. An official representative of the new president was there, too, and a whole carload of cabinet officers. Times had certainly changed in Portugal!

When Lucia arrived in Fatima, the Bishop of Leiria came down to meet her. Twenty-five years ago he had sent her away from there with the faint hope that she could forget all about the Cova da Iria. Now he wanted to say Mass there for her.

He had asked her to come for a special reason. In 1930, after eight years of official investigation, the good, cautious bishop had finally declared "worthy of belief, the visions of the shepherd children in the Cova da Iria, parish of Fatima, in this diocese, from the thirteenth of May to the thirteenth of October, 1917".

As far as the bishop knew, all available facts of the case were in by now. Not for five years did he suddenly realize how mistaken he might be! In 1935, when Jacinta's body was brought back to Fatima, her coffin was opened. To the amazement of the bishop—to the joy of Ti Marto and Tia Olimpia—Jacinta was found to be absolutely unchanged. She lay there as though she were asleep, her face untouched by the hand of disease or of death. Her cheeks were faintly pink, her body as fragrant as the field flowers that she had loved so dearly. It was an incredible sight—so moving that the bishop had the sleeping face photographed. He sent a copy of the picture to Lucia.

When Lucia saw it, the memories of her beloved cousin flooded through her heart like a spring torrent. She wrote to thank the bishop for the picture, and in doing so, she let slip a few hitherto unknown facts about her little cousin's last year of life. The bishop was struck by an alarming thought. Was there more to these seemingly simple children than anyone suspected? Had the self-effacing nun held back the *real* story of the children of Aljustrel just because no one had ever asked her to tell it?

The bishop ordered Lucia to write her recollections of everything in any way relating to that summer of 1917. Lucia had to turn out four manuscripts before he was satisfied that she had told him everything. Not until 1941 was the difficult job finished.

Lucia's memoirs gave the first full account of the hidden lives led by the three shepherds so many years ago—the inner life that they had kept so carefully guarded from their own people—their zeal for sacrifice, their secret conversations, the prophetic visions of Jacinta. In one of these documents she described for the first time the vision of hell that they had been shown in July. In another she casually let fall the information that an angel had appeared to them three times in 1916.

It was all too much for paper alone. The bishop decided that Lucia had better come home and go over all the ground mentioned in her memoirs in order to point out exactly where everything had happened. Besides that, the good man thought, it was only fair that she should be allowed to see what had been happening in Fatima lately.

Thus Lucia came to make another pilgrimage to all the places she loved. But what a happy pilgrimage it was this time! In Aljustrel she visited her sisters, and her beloved Aunt and Uncle Marto. She met a whole new flock of nephews and nieces. She took the bishop's representative—a younger, sprier man than the bishop—all over the countryside, pointing out to him the places she had written about. She showed him the rock from which the sheep had drunk the cool water after Francisco and Jacinta had refused it. She showed him the spots where the angel had appeared—by the well and on the hill. She went again to the sweet green field of Valinhos where the Lady had come to them in August. She prayed by the tomb of Francisco and Jacinta, whom the Pope would later be asked to canonize. She knelt once more before the altar where she had made her First Communion.

Back in the Cova da Iria, she stood by the Chapel of the Apparitions and thought of the wild, rocky field where three children had once built a playhouse of stone. There was joy, but there was also regret in the smile with which she looked around her—at the shining, white basilica that stood on the crown of the hill, at the hospital where sick pilgrims were cared for, at the religious houses, the new seminary, the great gates that flanked the entrance to the Cova, the fountain discovered, many people said, by a miracle.

"How much has happened here in twenty-five years!" she thought.

How much had happened to *her* in twenty-five years!

And now it was all done! Her work was finished. She had seen the Lady's wishes carried out. She had told all she knew about the lives of two future saints. She had patiently allowed herself to be questioned and questioned and questioned by an unending procession of authors. She had rendered a unique service to her Lady and to the world by acting as adviser to the American Dominican sculptor Father Thomas McGlynn, whose new statue of Our Lady of Fatima would soon stand over the door of the basilica itself. It was easy to see why God had wanted her available for all these years in the happy household of the Dorotheans.

But now, she asked her bishop, now that the job was done, could she please do what she had never for one minute stopped wanting to do? Now could she be a Carmelite?

And of course he agreed.

There was only one piece of unfinished business. That last secret! It was still to be reckoned with, and Lucia was still the only person in the world who knew what it was. A kind of legend has grown up around the final secret from Fatima. One heard that a copy of it was in the hands of the Holy Father, that he had read it, that our Lady herself had set the day of revelation for 1960, and so on.

At some point before she went into the Carmelites,

Lucia told the bishop that there was no longer any reason why she should not reveal the secret, and that, if he wanted her to, she was perfectly free to do so at once. The bishop most definitely did *not* want her to do so, as he assured her at once. Her last memoir had given him all the startling revelations he needed for some time to come. The secret was just one little responsibility he felt he could do without. The whole business had worn him out.

This was perfectly all right, too, Lucia told him. There was no pressing need to reveal the secret now. She would simply write it out and put it in an envelope and give it to him. Then, in case of her sudden illness or sudden death, there would be no cause for alarm.

Lucia lived in the Carmelite convent at Coimbra. When she retired forever behind the iron grille that separates Carmel from the world, she once again took a new name. This one was of her own choosing. She became Sister Maria of the Immaculate Heart.

Lucia disappeared from the view of the world. But the Lady for whose cause she fought so valiantly has covered it from one end to the other. From Greenland to Antarctica, from Alaska to Australia, from Bombay to San Francisco, from Saint Peter's in Rome to the smallest missionary chapel in Mozambique, the story of the Lady and the three shepherd children is told, and the Immaculate Heart of Mary is loved and honored. The Lady from Fatima—that tiny speck on the map of the little country—has captured the heart and the imagination of the

Catholic world to a degree unique in the history of the Church.

It would be impossible even to guess at the number of people who honor Our Lady of Fatima by saying her own prayer at the end of every decade of the Rosary, and by receiving Communion on the first Saturday of every month. She has an enormous, an uncountable number of friends today—perhaps because she chose her first three friends so well.

Author's Note

History is filled with wonderful events that have left discouragingly few or undependable written records behind them. We have to piece them together with guesswork and question marks. This is not true of the Fatima story. What happened there happened so recently, as history goes, that many of the people involved are still alive, and the whole story has been investigated by many excellent writers using the most modern methods of scholarly research.

Of the many books written about Fatima, I found the indispensable source to be *The Immaculate Heart* by Father John De Marchi (Farrar, Straus and Young, 1952), who spent so many years tracking down the minutest details of the story at its source. I am also indebted to George Boehrer and Costa Brochado's *Fatima: In the Light of History* (Milwaukee: Bruce, 1954) for a searching account of the Portuguese political scene and for a fascinating survey of the newspaper coverage given to our Lady's appearances in the Cova da Iria.

The charming incident related on page 110 was found in April Oursler Armstrong's *Fatima: Pilgrimage to Peace* (Garden City), which also contains valuable information on Sister Lucia's attitude toward the treatment accorded her father by writers on Fatima.

I would also like to thank the two Paul Humes for their valuable assistance, both critical and clerical, in getting the manuscript together.

Afterword

The year 1960 came and went, and still the third secret was not revealed. Lucia's handwritten account of the third secret, which she had entrusted to the Bishop of Leiria in 1944, was delivered to Pope John XXIII in August 1959. But the envelope remained sealed, unread by the Pope, and yet to be disclosed. Pope Paul VI read the secret in 1965, but he also did not reveal the secret to the world. Years later, Pope John Paul II read Lucia's letter describing the third secret, shortly after the assassination attempt on his life. It was many decades after our Lady's apparitions to the three shepherd children at Fatima that the third secret was shared with the world, and our Lady's wish for Russia to be consecrated to her Immaculate Heart was fulfilled.

Cardinal Angelo Sodano, on behalf of Pope John Paul II, revealed the message of the third secret in Fatima in May 2000. The third part of our Lady's message—which, as Lucia's letter recounts, followed the vision of hell and our Lady's predictions of much suffering and war unless people repented and Russia was converted—was a vision. In this vision, an angel appeared proclaiming "Penance, Penance, Penance". Then the children saw a man in white, whom they recognized to be a pope. Many bishops, priests, and religious men and women joined this pope; these holy people struggled to climb a mountain, at the top of which stood a cross. The pope appeared to be in much pain and sorrow for the souls of dead people he saw on his journey to the cross. When the Church leaders, in the company of other people too, reached the top of the mountain, they were attacked by soldiers with arrows and bullets, and they were killed. The vision ended with two angels at the foot of the cross, who sprinkled the souls of the dead with blood from the martyrs.

Vatican officials explain that the suffering of the Church leaders in the vision represent the martyrs who have been persecuted for the Church throughout the century, especially those who have died in the two World Wars and smaller wars across the world. It is also believed that the vision in part predicted the assassination attempt on Pope John Paul II's life, when he was shot in 1981. The Pope himself attributed his escape from death on that thirteenth day of May to Our Lady of Fatima. And in 1991, he brought the bullet that wounded him to Fatima, where it was placed in the crown on her statue.

Lucia de Santos lived out her years quietly in the Carmelite convent at Coimbra, where she died on the thirteenth of February 2005. Pope John Paul II consecrated the world to the Immaculate Heart of Mary in a speech in 1984, invoking especially "those individuals and nations that particularly need to be thus entrusted and consecrated". Lucia lived to see the end of communism in Russia; to witness the beatification of Francisco and Jacinta in 2000; and to hear the Church reveal our Lady's last message of penance and vision of suffering, which the children of Fatima had experienced so many years before.

— EMILY ZOMBERG AYALA